Another Side of Armageddon

Judgment In Time Series Book IV

New People Publishing

Follow us on Facebook and Twitter to keep up with
Judgment In Time conversations and updates

Facebook: www.facebook.com \ JITSeries
Twitter: @JITSeries

Available in Hardcover, Paperback, and
eBook as ePub, Kindle, and Nook

Fiction: Action and Adventure, Political Intrigue, Alternative History, Romance, Mystery, Thriller, Time Travel, Historical Fiction, Military Fiction, Science Fiction, Naval Battles

Judgment In Time Series

New People Publishing
www.NewPeoplePublishing.com

Editor: Robert Allen Fisher
Cover Art and Full Page Illustrations: Jennifer Cole
Production Design and Illustrations: Tom Hultgren

ISBN-13: 978-0-9990580-3-9
Advance Edition: Trade Paperback

Printed in the United States of America by:
Lightning Source

10 9 8 7 6 5 4 3 2 1

About the Author

Kevin Klesert, a successful independent businessman, has experienced firsthand how small businesses all over the country carried a disproportionate amount of the burden to meet their legal obligations. The steady erosion of Main Street USA under mountains of onerous regulations, licenses, taxes, and fees from Federal, State, and Local Governments have all but destroyed their ability to succeed and turn a reasonable profit.

His intense study of historical trends brought to him the correlation between the downfall of dominant societies of the past and the current struggle to maintain the most noble and ambitious political experiment in human history, the United States of America. He discovered the seeds of ruin were planted within the very generation that launched the United States to world preeminence.

Kevin Klesert's desire to shed light on this dire situation through the means of a thrilling adventure has produced a story worthy of the fight against these negative forces. The ideas for the Judgment In Time Series percolated in his adventurous imagination while he raised his four children and ran an award-winning design and construction company. A 3rd generation native of Southern California, Kevin Klesert imbues his writing with his passion for history, adventure, and fantasy.

Table of Contents

Characters

Enterprise Task Force Main Characters

Rear Admiral UH Retired Sean Phillips – Former Commanding Officer, Enterprise Task Force

Captain Anthony Knox – Taíno God Yúcahu & later Tactical Adjunct to Admiral Sean Phillips

Rear Admiral UH Retired Alicia Calhoun – Former Secretary of Defense

Captain Renée Aslan – Former Naval Attaché to Alicia Calhoun

Captain Carl Eddington – Commanding Officer, battleship USS Missouri

Dr. Rebecca Cutler Eddington, PhD – Comstock Technologies Lead Specter Engineer

Enterprise Task Force Support Characters

Captain Daniel Osaka – Commanding Officer, carrier USS Enterprise

Captain Mark Daily – attack submarine USS Seawolf

Captain *Dash* Nelson – Air Wing Commander [CAG], USS Enterprise

Captain Tobias Harris – Deputy Air Wing Commander [DCAG]

Commander Logan Barrish – destroyer USS Decatur

Commander Andy Gable – cargo ship USNS Amelia Earhart

Lt. Commander Maria Brizuela – fleet oiler USNS Patuxent

Lt. Gloria Layworth – Bridge Communications Officer, USS Enterprise

Commander Michael *Thorny* Thornton – Task Force SEAL Commander

Commander Wesley Brenner – Executive Officer USS Seawolf

Captain Henry Jackson – cruiser USS Shiloh

Captain Randy Stone – Seahawk Pilot on USS Shiloh

Senior Civilian Officer Bradley Franks – fleet oiler USNS Patuxent

Dr. Forrest Phelps, PhD – Comstock Technologies Computer Specialist

Yacahuey – Interpreter for Taíno God Yúcahu, Captain Anthony Knox

Supernatural Characters

Darius – Carl Eddington, Aaron's Father, Sean Anthony's Father

Durius – Aaron's Mother, Ex-wife to Darius

Cromulus – Jesus

Advanced Entity Impersonating Benjamin Franklin

Advanced Entity Impersonating Various David Bowie Personas

Characters Continued

Additional Ship Captains

Captain Gordon Lincoln – cruiser USS Princeton

Captain Frederick Johnson – cruiser USS Chancellorsville

Captain Marlowe Turner – attack submarine USS Hampton

Commander Jonathan James – attack Submarine USS Indiana

Commander Regis Goddard – destroyer USS John Paul Jones

Commander Melissa Wu – cargo ship USNS Cesar Chavez

Lt. Commander James Peck – fleet oiler USNS Laramie

1492 Reality Support Characters

Pope Alexander VI

Toms de Torquemada – Spanish Inquisition Inquisitor General

Henry VII and Elizabeth – King and Queen of England

2018 Reality Main Characters

Sean Anthony Eddington – Advanced Entity, Son of Carl and Rebecca

Phoenix – Black Hat Hacker

Adonis – Black Hat Hacker

President Susan Harrison

Aaron Fletcher – Advanced Entity, Chief of Staff to President Harrison

2018 Reality Support Characters

Sarah Whineglaus – Secretary to the President

Tom Abernathy – Assistant Secretary to the President

Vice President Simon Fredericks

General Addison – Commanding Officer, US Strategic Command

General Favors – Air Force Chief of Staff

General Leigh – Commanding Officer, US Northern Command

Sergei Romanov – Russian Prime Minister

Captain Harris – 160th Infantry Regiment, California National Guard

Colonel Valerie Brighten – US Army Brigade Commander

Frederick Masterson – Business Tycoon

Morris Zagruder – Business Tycoon

The Grey

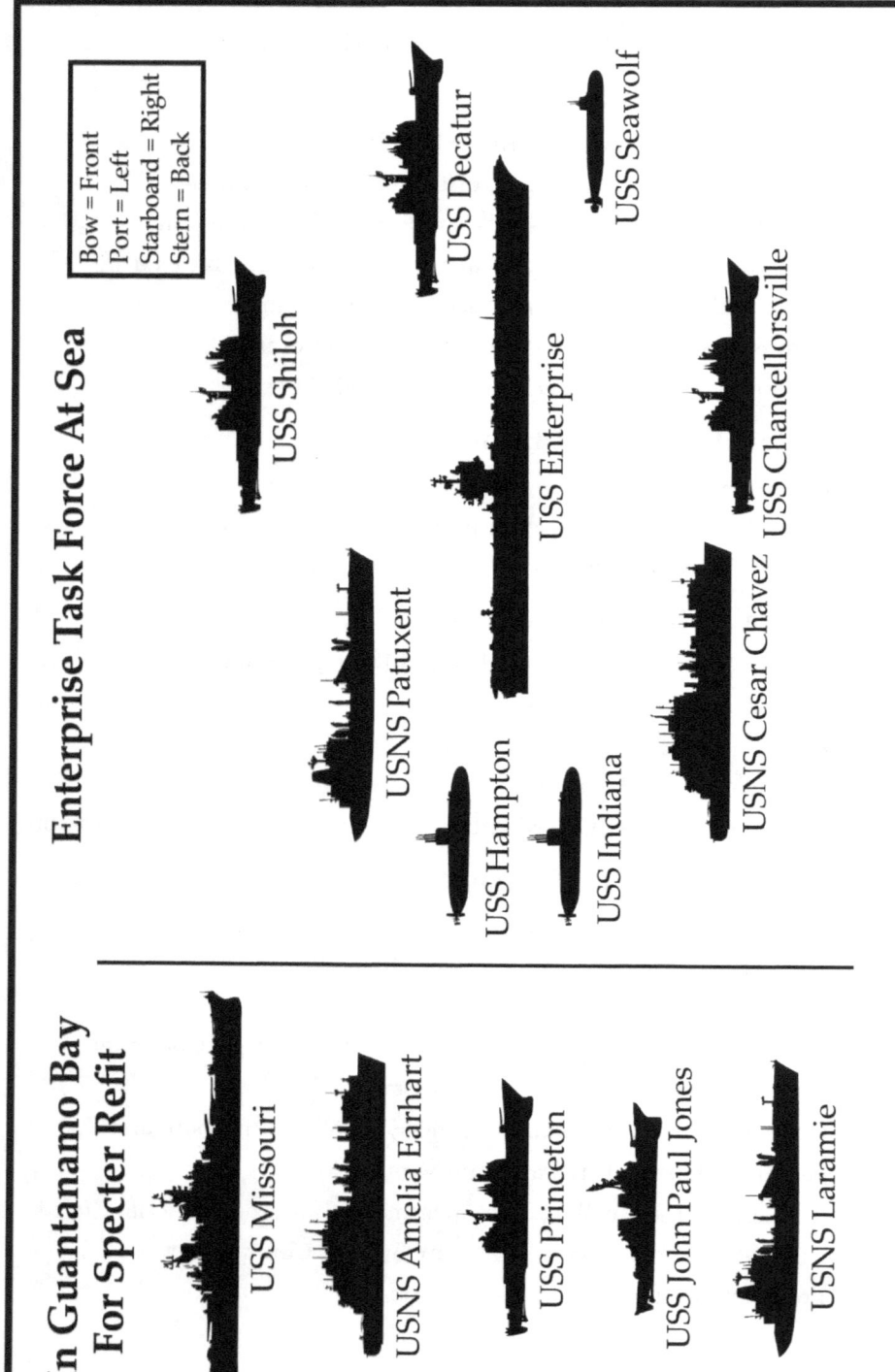

Part I
Batshit Crazy

Taíno Symbol for Water

With their private moment ruined, Tony and Renée didn't have the time to consider the bad choices Franklin had presented, because Sean and Alicia burst into the room. After a quick round of hugs celebrating their narrow escape, Sean got down to business.

"I ordered the attack flights to return, but we are maintaining a CAP [Combat Air Patrol] over eastern Cuba. So far, all preliminary after action reports state we didn't suffer any serious casualties, so for once it looks like I will not have to perform any services. Also for the first time, we didn't suffer any battle damage, except for the usual technical wear and tear of combat. I ordered the task force on a course to the last known coordinates of the Nazi task force, which is a little over one hundred miles to the southeast. Search and rescue is underway for any downed Nazi pilots."

Finished with the after action report, Sean plopped down on the couch as Alicia handed him a glass of wine. "And, I am sorry to add, but because of the risk of further attacks from unknowns, it is too risky to transfer you and Renée to the Missouri for now. You will have to wait until we get closer to Guantanamo Bay. I have asked Captain Osaka to arrange quarters for you here, but I doubt any of us will get much sleep tonight."

"And much to our enjoyment," Alicia added with sarcasm, "we received another visit from Bowie."

"It must have been while Franklin visited us," Renée added.

A knock at the door interrupted, which resulted in another round of hugs, kisses, and well wishes that they were all still alive when a more effusive than usual Rebecca bounded into the room.

"I had this fantastic conversation in my head with Carl, and let me tell you..." was all Rebecca could get out before Sean interrupted.

"Dr. Cutler, we have all just entertained ethereal visitors, so for now may I suggest we all take some time to relax. We can discuss our encounters later over dinner." This sounded more like an order than a suggestion.

"Agreed," Tony seconded, as he poured tumblers of Jack Daniels Single Barrel. "Anyone else want a real drink?"

As promised, after dinner and everyone had shared their encounters with Bowie, Franklin, and Carl, they all came to the same conclusion. Their only real option would be to commit the task force to a voyage across the Atlantic.

"Over 10,000 sailors under our command and all we can offer them in the way of hope is to cross the Atlantic in an attempt to stop getting shot at, convert an entire continent to our way of thinking, and, oh, return in one piece." Once again Tony's sarcasm lightened the mood.

True to his nature, Sean felt compelled to understand the why of it. "So to sum up the situation, we have two supernatural entities masquerading as David Bowie and Benjamin Franklin. Rebecca's husband Captain Carl Eddington residing in Specter, and powers of unknown origin who feel it is important enough to change the course of two separate, yet mirror image realities. Why 1942 and 1492 for starters?"

Tony was quick to respond. "1492 is the easy one. Think about how different the world would be if it was the other way around and the Western Hemisphere conquered Europe instead. Sweat lodges, cliff dwellings instead of suburban tracts, living off the land, respect for nature, and – wait a minute; I think I could live with that."

"Instead," Renée interjected, "ninety percent of the indigenous population wiped out, those of a different ethnic makeup imported in as slaves, and all kneeled down to the god of greed and corruption. Without the riches stolen from the Americas, Spain, France, and England could not have afforded the wars of the next three centuries, or fueled the conquest of Asia and India. Seems to me, if there was ever any chance to change the barbaric nature of man, 1492 ended that dream for good. Keeping Europe out for our, as promised, elongated lifetimes might be enough to even the odds."

Though impressed with Renée's passion, her solution failed to satisfy Sean. "Interesting ideas Renée. However, I don't know about anyone else, but I am tired of not having any control over what happens next. Besides, it still doesn't answer the why."

Alicia laughed. "Like we had any choices before. Correct me if I am wrong, but isn't this how it worked all along? We of all people know the cost you pay for standing up for what is right over what will put money in your pockets. All of us had the choice of being rich and powerful at the expense of our souls."

Renée agreed. "Exactly, and that is why, regardless of who pulls the strings, the best we can do is to live up to our ideals of how life should be. We don't need to understand motives we are not privy to, so why not simply do it because it is the right thing to do?"

Alicia nodded her agreement. "If I remember correctly, that was the same attitude we took in 1942, and it served us well then. Speaking of which, as the one who spent time in 1942 after we left, Tony should know the importance of that year."

"Enlighten us, oh mighty Anthony." Renée made a flourish to

exaggerate her words.

"Simple enough, smart-ass. If our country had any sense of righteousness after winning WWII, instead of the empty promises of liberty and justice for all that followed, I doubt we would be here. The ones moving us around probably came to this conclusion and said enough of this shit. Both moments in time brought about the hypocrisy of Western moral superiority."

Tony's friends sat in shocked silence.

"What?" he asked, stunned by their response.

Alicia felt obligated to share the obvious. "No offense, Tony, but I think I can speak for all of us when I say that was the most philosophical thought we have ever heard come out of your mouth." Alicia had to suppress a smile throughout her assessment of her now embarrassed friend's comments.

Seeing the rare hurt expression on her lover's face, Renée went in for the kill. "You have to admit that you are always the first to grab for the Scotch the minute anyone tries to rationalize a current crisis in the context of past offenses."

"Beats waiting for the next joker to come along and hit us with a particle ray beam." To the amazement of everyone in the room, the now truculent Tony walked over to the bar and grabbed the Scotch, which brought out another round of laughter. After looking at them and then at the bottle in his hand, he too joined in.

When the room calmed down, Rebecca added her opinion. "Then there is this to think about. What exactly would we be returning to if we did go back home now? As much as I grew up cloistered in the scientific community until all of this madness began, I for one love all the wonderful paradoxes our adventures have supplied. How could any of us ever go back to normal, especially if that normal included entering another Dark Age?"

Alicia chuckled at Rebecca's take on their situation. "Unfair comparison Rebecca; you were born for crazy."

Sean knew they still needed to convince the crews, but with the bait being an elongated lifetime, he didn't think that would be a problem. "All right, then if we are going to Europe, Tony and Renée will have to come with us. Tony, I will need you to become my Chief of Staff so I can have my wife back."

Alicia immediately objected. "Like my opinion doesn't matter? Since when did you speak for me?"

It quickly dawned on Sean that he had not thought this through, and the icy stare from Alicia drove that point home. Sean reached out to Tony with his eyes to help save his ass.

After the thrashing he had just gone through, Tony smiled and sank further into the couch to watch the show. The look said it all. "Son, you're on your own."

Bravely, Sean attempted to defend himself. "I thought it would allow you more freedom to think outside of the box if you were not tied to the nuts and bolts of the fleet."

Bad move. "Okay, so now you are saying that I can't chew gum and walk at the same time?"

Thoroughly defeated, Sean gave up. With the right amount of contrition in his voice, he leaned close and whispered in her ear, "I didn't mean to belittle you. I should have asked you beforehand. My bad, will not happen again."

"It was more how you stated it, than the content tiger." She gave Sean her most wicked smile, while purring the words, "You can have your balls back now."

Sean leaned back. "Well then, Tony I still need you to perform your usual brilliance with the tactical planning."

"Whatever you need from either me or Renée, we would both be honored to oblige for this trip only. When we return to Cuba, Renée and I want to be together to help the Taíno."

"Speaking of responsibilities, don't you think it is time that you include me on the list somewhere? After all, Carl and I did manage world affairs after you and Alicia returned home."

As much as Rebecca made a good point, the last thing Sean

wanted to do right now was give the scientist any formal rank or position, partly because of her relationship with the mysterious Carl Eddington. "I'm sorry Rebecca, I thought you were more comfortable working out the scientific aspects and would have looked at any additional tasks as unnecessary distractions. What exactly do you have in mind? The rank of Commander?"

"Oh no, you are absolutely correct. Could you imagine me trying to give an order?"

Tony thought of the perfect role. "I know, we can put her in charge of new uniforms when ours wear out. What do you think of pastels and prints instead of fatigues? We can use hair dyes instead of patches to differentiate ranks. How does red work for you, Sean?"

After the laughter once again died down, Alicia interjected. "How about you continue to save our asses with your immense brain, and when we get to Europe you work with me on the diplomatic end. More like the Deputy Secretary of State."

"It is settled then," Sean hoped. He realized the humor masked the reality that they all had almost died, and that thousands of others had died. "Let's get down to what needs to be done here while we are gone. Renée, coordinate with Commander Gable regarding the establishment of the onshore settlement. We will also need someone to interact with the Taíno. Rebecca, we will need…"

Tony interrupted. "It would be better if Renée and I meet with Yacahuey. I can convince him that it is important for the Taíno to help Commander Gable protect them from any further attacks."

"Good point. Back to you Rebecca. We need an update on how long it will take to complete the Specter upgrades on the Princeton, John Paul Jones, Missouri, Laramie, and Amelia Earhart."

"First off, Deputy Secretary of State sounds groovy, and the only thing that can hold me up is access to the ships and enough qualified engineers to do the work."

"Why don't you and Dr. Phelps get going on that now?"

"Yes Sir, Admiral, Sir." After a deep bow, Rebecca spun around, and was gone.

"Tony, work out with Commander Thornton how to get control of those Nazi supply ships without any damages and hopefully any further casualties. At this point, there shouldn't be any fight left in them, but who knows. As soon as we are in range…"

"Light 'em up," Tony interrupted. "Not really much of a plan needed. They'll take one look of Thorny's smiling black face hanging out of the door of the Seahawk and shit their pants."

Sean needed Tony to take the threat seriously. "Look, who knows how far they went creating their ideal Master Race, so make sure the crew of those supply ships don't know what hit them. If a few of them need to die to protect our people, so be it. Also, make sure enough interpreters go with the SEALs just in case."

Itching for some action, Tony had to ask, "You want me to ride along?"

"Hell no."

On his way out the door, Tony complained. "You're no fun."

"Alicia, I need you to coordinate with the Marines about how to secure the Nazi crews on whichever of our ships would be best suited after we relieve them of their duties. Remember, security over comfort as they will be offloaded as soon as we reach Guantanamo."

"On it." After a quick kiss, Alicia exited, leaving Sean alone.

"Why did I think I had any control over any of this?" he thought before he too left to fill in Captain Osaka on the bridge.

When the Seahawks with Commander Thornton's SEALs arrived at the location of the remnants of the Nazi task force, they boarded the Nazi supply ships with such speed, there wasn't any question of the crews offering resistance. Most were still in shock over the devastation they had witnessed hours earlier. The commandos quickly discovered most of the crew had taken the ships over from their Nazi officers. After the interpreters interviewed all the rescued survivors, they found that most were Americans, spoke English, and rejoiced at their release from their Nazi overlords.

With the rest of the Nazi survivors pulled from the water and the supply ships secured, the task force changed their course back to Guantanamo Bay. As planned, the first order of business was to round up the hard-core SS type Nazi officers and bring them aboard the Decatur, which then split from the group and headed to the deserted Navassa Island. Left at the mercy of the elements, they would have the opportunity to discover exactly how superior their race was.

A few hours later, Sean returned to the Admirals Quarters to consider the fate of the hardline Nazis. After receiving reports about the brutality of their actions from the supply ship crews, he knew he would not lose a second of sleep worrying about them. Though he feigned indifference, the recognition that this evil existed in him always created a momentary crisis of faith. "How many deaths are on my hands?" Lost in thought about how easy it is to justify with complete confidence condemning those whose sole purpose in life was the eradication of entire ethnic groups, Sean didn't hear the knock on the door.

In the back of his mind, the words "Are you all right, Admiral?" broke him out of his reverie.

"Come in, Renée."

"Am I interrupting you, Sir?"

Sean could see the concern in her face, so he quickly buried his thoughts and gave her a smile. "No Renée, I was day dreaming. Anyway, what can I do for you?"

"Not my place to pry," Renée reasoned to herself. "I came to fill you in on some interesting news I discovered while communicating with Commander Gable."

"First off Renée, whenever we are in an informal setting, Sean will be fine. Please, have a seat."

"Yes Sir," Renée acknowledged. "It seems Commander Gable has a Taíno scholar under his command named Lt. Commander Maria Brizuela, and it turns out she had some interesting information to share."

"Brizuela, what an interesting name. Where does she hail from?" Sean asked.

"The name dates back to a Taíno cacique, or chief, named Brizuela of Baitiquirí, which is on the coast about twelve miles east of the entrance to Guantanamo Bay. According to history, he is ruling there now. She has studied the Taíno as well as the history of all the pre-Columbian peoples of the Western Hemisphere since she was 9 years old."

Sean shook his head in disbelief. "Correct me if I'm wrong, but isn't it an incredible stroke of good luck to have someone so versed in an almost completely lost culture right here in our midst?"

To Sean this sounded like something Bowie or Franklin would have dreamed up. "Are you sure she is for real?"

Renée was quick with the answer. "I checked and double checked her story. The Lt. Commander completed her Master's Degree in American Indian Studies at the University of Arizona in Tucson before joining the Navy to pay for it. She currently commands the Patuxent, and Commander Gable has a Lt. Commander on the Amelia Earhart, who previously commanded a fleet oiler, to take over her ship.

"Further, I suggest we comb the task force for personnel who might possess similar interests to help develop the Taíno into ambassadors who can reach out to the tribes throughout the Americas. It also might help if we took some Taíno with us to experience the people of Europe. Right now, all they know is some men in wooden ships came from somewhere and they killed them because their god Tony said to. Wouldn't it be better if some of their people with firsthand knowledge reported the dangers they face?"

Sean liked the idea, so he gave Renée a quick nod. "Go ahead and coordinate the details with Commander Gable and Tony. Also, we won't be back at Guantanamo Bay until sometime tonight, so tell Alicia to schedule a staff meeting for tomorrow at 1300 hours."

"Yes Sir. Also, Alicia informed me that we rescued seventy-five Nazi survivors, who are now secured on the aft deck of the Patuxent. Initial interrogations have revealed they were every bit in the dark as us, and their SS handlers were positively scared shitless when they lost contact with the fatherland. The Americans among them were more than helpful and could be a real help in building the settlement."

Sean wasn't so confident. "All it takes is one to screw it all up. For now we will treat them as prisoners of war until we return from Europe. If they still want to help under this arrangement, I want armed guards supervising their every movement."

Sean had one more important message he needed Renée to convey. "Inform Tony and Alicia that Commander Andy Gable is due a promotion. I am increasing his rank to Captain, and I want him to assume command of the Guantanamo base. Further, since we are giving Lt. Commander Brizuela greater responsibilities, I am increasing her rank to Commander. They will report directly to you until we depart."

The phone rang before Renée could respond. Sean motioned for her to hold on as he picked it up. "Yes? Come right up. Thank you."

"Anything else Renée?"

No, thank you, Admiral. I'll get back with Alicia now, and pass your orders on to Tony."

"Sean, remember?"

"Sorry Sir. As long as I am aboard an American warship, and you are in command, it will be Admiral, Sir." Renée followed with a stiff salute that Sean returned with a smile.

A few minutes after Renée left, there was another knock on the door.

"Come in, Rebecca."

Not yet all the way through the door, Rebecca was in full report mode. "Including sea trials, we can have all the ships converted in 2 weeks if we don't do the Amelia Earhart, and if the new supply ships are going, then add another two weeks. And can we rename them in the tradition of our ships?"

Sean took a moment to think through different scenarios they might run into before deciding. "They may need to travel by sea to another location while we are gone, so having the Amelia Earhart cloaked would be an asset. Specter upgrades on all ships including the Nazi supply ships. Also, I will take your suggestion to rename the new supply ships under advisement. Keep me updated with your progress."

"Of course Admiral," Rebecca acknowledged on her way out the door.

Admiral Sean Phillips in his dress whites looked every bit the commander he was as he stared at the men and women seated around the conference table. After an hour of sometimes heated discussions with his senior commanders, his final decision on the near future of his ships and crew was at hand. After a quick nod to Tony and Alicia, he dove in.

"It has become abundantly clear to me that if we continue to let events dictate our fate, we are doomed to extinction through attrition. Therefore, I am ordering this group to split into two, one led by Captain Daily of the Seawolf to the English Channel and the other formed around the Enterprise to the Mediterranean Sea.

"Our mission will be to impose our will on the ruling structures of the 15th Century. Though there are many Catholics and Christians serving under us, the history of the church in this era is not one anyone here would recognize or want to defend.

"Once the Enterprise arrives in the Mediterranean, we will seek out and modify the Roman Catholic Church's understanding of their duties to the people, as well as end the rule of King John II of Portugal, and Queen Isabella I and King Ferdinand II of Spain.

"Captain Daily, you will lead your forces against King Henry VII of England, King James IV of Scotland, and King John I of Denmark-Norway. Our objective is to institute a complete restructuring of Europe's political and economic policies."

Three of the staff officers became uncomfortable in their seats, which drew Tony's attention. "Before you question our motives, remember I am also a reformed Catholic, and when I say reformed why not put it to the test right now. How many of you in this room think what the church has stood for in the Middle Ages represented a kind and loving god? No one in the 15th Century could question the church's power any more than we could in our time, with one major difference; they were burned at the stake when they tried."

Tony had a more developed perspective than those who were new to the experience of questioning a lifetime of dogma. "Look at it like God has given us all a much more up close and personal role in clearing the way for what It really wants."

Captain Daily only wanted to focus on the planning. The rest to him was all existential claptrap. "Why split our forces, Sir?"

Sean nodded to him in thanks. "Nothing more than maximizing our resources. We will leave the Missouri and the Amelia Earhart at Guantanamo Bay to work on our settlement. I will take the Enterprise with the Chancellorsville, John Paul Jones, Decatur, Cesar Chavez, Patuxent, Susquehanna, Indiana, and the Hampton into the Mediterranean, and Captain Daily, you will take the Seawolf, Shiloh, Princeton, Norman Schwarzkopf, and Laramie north up the coast to England, Scotland, and Denmark-Norway."

Something confused Captain Henry Jackson of the Shiloh. "Excuse me, Sir, but you listed the Susquehanna and the Norman Schwarzkopf. What ships are those?"

Alicia answered. "Upon recommendation, we renamed the Nazi oiler to USNS Susquehanna and the cargo ship to USNS Norman

Schwarzkopf. Apparently you didn't get the memo."

After a chuckle circled the room, the meeting continued for another two hours as they planned the logistics of the undertaking down to the smallest detail. When they finished, Sean had one last announcement. "I will address the crews in one hour. Dismissed."

After the last of the senior staff left to return to their commands, Captain Mark Daily of the Seawolf remained behind with Rebecca.

Mark wanted to satisfy his curiosity. "So what do you think Dr. Eddington? Do you believe Carl Eddington is sailing with us?"

Rebecca reacted to the wrong use of her name. "Awfully presumptive of you to assume that because I married and bore a child with Carl, that I would take his name."

"My bad. But when you're left in the dark about so many matters that impact your life, all you're left with *is* assumptions."

"Tell me about it."

"About Carl?"

"Carl is manipulating Specter's Command and Control, and that is what happened to the nuclear missile. He sent it somewhere else, and my best guess is somewhere in the middle of the Pacific. When Specter didn't show the same power spike it did when the Nazis showed up, it could only mean the power responsible was already here."

"And because of your dreams about Carl, you believe he is the only one capable?"

"If not him, then I hate to think of what else might be around to pull it off."

"For all of our sakes, I hope you're right, Dr. Cutler."

In conveying the choices to the sailors of the fleet, Sean avoided most of the existential aspects of the journey. In the orders he delivered throughout the task force over the ship intercoms, he first spoke to the sailors concerns about surviving in their new world. "Not one of you asked for this, but we're all in this together if we want to survive. The most important thing those of us who

14

Northern Group to England

Bow = Front
Port = Left
Starboard = Right
Stern = Back

USS Seawolf

USS Princeton

USS Shiloh

USNS Laramie

USNS Norman
Schwarzkopf
(Former Nazi Cargo Ship)

Remained in
Guantanamo Bay

USS Missouri

USNS Amelia Earhart

Captain Andy Gable
Guantanamo Base Commander
Commander Maria Brizuela
Commanding Officer
Indigenous Relations Command

Enterprise Group to the Mediterranean

Bow = Front
Port = Left
Starboard = Right
Stern = Back

USS Decatur

USS John Paul Jones

USS Hampton

USS Enterprise

USS Chancellorsville

USS Patuxent

USNS Susquehanna
(Former Nazi Fleet Oiler)

USNS Cesar Chavez

USS Indiana

Lt. Commander Michelle Chen
Replaced Commander Maria Brizuela
As Captain of USNS Patuxent

experienced this before can relay to you is this. As long as you stand by your mates and perform your duties as sailors of the finest naval force the world has ever seen, you will greatly enhance our odds of returning home in one piece. I can't promise that all will be sunshine and roses, you only have to remember the loss of the Churchill to see this isn't a game, and that real people's lives are on the line."

There wasn't any way Sean was going to expose Bowie and Franklin's promises if they went to Europe, so brutal honesty would have to suffice. "Rather than sit around and wait for the next attack, it has been decided that our best bet to return home lies in setting course to Europe. Continue to follow your orders and I will do my best to see all of us safely home. Admiral Phillips out."

By now, those who had experienced 1942 were liberally interspersed throughout the fleet and were quick to snuff out negative scuttlebutt and assuage any fears of those who still struggled with the idea. Later, as Sean read the reports, he was pleasantly surprised there was little dissension among the ranks. Most just wanted to get on with it.

Sarah Whineglaus could not believe how much had changed under the current tenant of the White House, and because of those changes, her home in Vermont was looking real nice right about now. In the twenty-five years she served as the President's Secretary, only under the second Bush did she feel for the first time that the downfall of civilization had a chance of occurring in her lifetime.

Her current boss, President Susan Harrison, was on the phone with the Chinese President selling out Taiwan. Only an hour before, the Japanese ambassador had stormed out after discovering the United States Navy had withdrawn to Pearl Harbor, which left the door wide open for China to send ultimatums to both South Korea and Japan to accept the New Asian Sphere of Influence. In other words, submit to Chinese rule or face destruction.

Sarah could only hope China didn't resort to nuclear weapons like the growing number of countries already had, including Pakistan, India, and of course the United States. "If the average American knew half of what I do, they would dig a hole, climb in, and bury themselves."

"What was that, Sarah"?

"Nothing, Tom."

"I have to stop thinking out loud," she mumbled.

Before Sarah could form another thought, her mind disconnected from her body, as a foreign presence pushed her identity into a corner. "Hello Sarah. Don't worry, I won't be staying long," Phoenix soothed.

Being a devout Christian, Sarah panicked and tried to scream out for her lord and savior to throw the demon out; however, this demon had other plans.

It took all of Phoenix's will to keep the transformation from looking like an epileptic attack. "Sorry to disappoint you Sarah, but Jesus isn't available right now. Relax I'm not a demon, and if you settle down, I promise you won't remember anything after I'm gone."

Phoenix opened Sarah's mind to the happiest past life she had lived, a life where Charles Darwin was her son. For the first time in years, a peace of mind she had rarely realized permeated her consciousness. Her face would have glowed if she had any control over her body.

With Sarah off in her other life and Phoenix in full control of her body, it didn't take long to set up access to Sarah's computer.

Sean Anthony's now wide-awake hackers downloaded tons of data and uploaded a virus Phoenix developed that would worm its way from the White House network to the NSA server hub.

Phoenix went deep into Sarah's memories to access all the pertinent data from the President Harrison's first term. For good measure, she also dug into Sarah's memories of the President's predecessors for context, getting in and out in less than five minutes. "Thank you, little Miss Sarah. Now might be the time to move full time into that cabin you built in the Adirondack Mountains, because from the look of things, your current position is not long for this world. See you soon."

Sarah's head snapped back and she almost flew out of her chair. "Did you hear that?" she shouted to her assistant Tom.

"Hear what? The President is still on the phone and all is quiet here." He looked away so she would not see the look of disdain on his face. "It looks like the old battle-ax is finally losing it."

After Phoenix entered the data from her foray into Sarah's mind, it took another hour for the hackers to put the big picture together, and for Sean Anthony to hit upon the perfect counter. It turned out he was not alone, as he and Phoenix blurted out in unison, "Frederick Masterson!"

Before Sean Anthony could explain why, Phoenix beat him to it. "He's perfect. Creator of the world's next generation of operating systems, worth more than God, every bit the power-obsessed megalomaniac as Aaron, and fortunately for us, he is also in my lineage. According to our research, he gave more corporate bundled dark money to Aaron's cause than anyone else."

"It's hack attack time," Sean Anthony said, as he pulled one of the empty chairs up to her workstation. At least that was what Phoenix thought they were going to do. Instead, Sean Anthony suddenly disappeared and reappeared with his face on her monitor.

"Why would you put yourself in there?"

Sean Anthony skipped right past her question. "Mr. Masterson, remember you're him."

"Fine, be that way."

"Now, please."

Phoenix was familiar with this side of Sean Anthony. He liked to give her the room to put the pieces together without all the facts. "Just remember, what goes around, comes around," she chided.

He certainly hoped so. "It's good to have you back as you. Now can you focus, please?"

"All right, already. It would be much easier to focus if you would be quiet," Phoenix reprimanded, before she slipped into a trance fully prepared for another round of freak out. To her surprise once she entered the megalomaniac's mind, Masterson was completely at home with this invasion of his thoughts. Her first impressions of this version of herself left a sour taste. "I'm a fricking sociopath."

"Do you know a better way to truly live free?" Masterson replied. "Because if you found another way to live in this world with complete freedom of movement without first buying the right, let me know. By the way, how are you doing this? Have you developed a device to implant thoughts directly into my brain? If it is, you have my attention."

Phoenix immediately realized trying to push his mind aside was not an option. "Look, how about you taking a backseat for a moment and let me do my thing."

"Why would I let anyone dictate to me? From what I can read of you, it seems we share the same interests, so why don't you get out of my head and make an appointment to share your thoughts in, shall we say a more conventional manner?"

"That's it. I don't have time for this shit." Phoenix opened her mind so Masterson could see the full scope of his lives, leaving him much too busy to worry about what she wanted to do.

Once she achieved complete control, Sean Anthony appeared on the computer monitor on Masterson's desk. The office they found themselves in couldn't be more garish if filled with velvet nudes. Unfortunately, with his memories now belonging to her, it brought new meaning to where the leather on the couch, and the materials in the carpet had originated. "Sick twisted bastard. Can I cut this part out of me, please?"

"Another time, sweetie. Call in your secretary, and let's corrupt some files."

⚜

Admiral Sean Phillips nerves were on edge. Five days had passed since he issued the command to split his forces, and not one single threat appeared on the task force radars. There was little activity on the flight deck this late at night, outside of the two F-35 Lightnings on ready alert. He stood in front of the forward port catapult and stared out at the empty ocean. It was a chilly, cloudless night, and he could clearly see the running lights of the John Paul Jones a quarter mile ahead.

"I can't blame you for being pensive. Personally, I thought something perfectly nasty would have occurred when you sent half your force to my island home."

Sean didn't bother to turn around. "So are you here to lay on me the secrets of the universe, or to blow more smoke up my ass?"

"I'll tell you what. I will keep the smoke to a limit if you explain why you don't believe toppling the power structure of Europe advances your goals, and I will tell you something you don't already know."

Sean turned around to see an older version of the apparition's Bowie impersonation, somewhere in his mid-fifties, his hair now silver, and his body covered in a floor-length wool overcoat with a knitted scarf wrapped around his neck. "So is this the older and wiser you that is supposed to engender trust in me?"

This understated version of Bowie removed a pack of cigarettes from his coat pocket, shook one out, and lit it. After taking a generous drag, he responded. "Trust is a tricky thing. You gave your oath to a government that now wants to kill you for faithfully carrying out that oath, so excuse me if I do not sympathize with your current predicament."

Sean laughed, and shook his head. "Give me one of your cigarettes." Bowie shook one out, and handed it the Sean. "You just don't get it. This is not about what I do or don't want. I am responsible for the other 10,000 plus sailors who care more about their next birthday party with the folks back home than any esoteric exercise in who should run the world. Most would fight for whoever feeds and houses them the best over someone who points out their lack of freedoms. A little sex, NFL on the TV, a shrimp on the barbi, a brewski, and bam, they are good. I doubt there are more than a couple hundred members under my command that can tell you who the King and Queen of Spain are, let alone how many people in the Americas they killed to steal their gold and their land. Not to mention corrupting the survivors with their religion. Remember American schools still teach that Columbus is a hero."

"If I didn't know better, I would think you have become quite cynical about the situation. That is if I didn't know that secretly you are having the time of your life."

Before Sean could disagree, Bowie wagged a finger, of no, no, no. "You can't claim bullshit. Both you and that simply divine Alicia spent years building up your vision of the perfect world, and here it is, right in front of you to mold as you wish. However, because of your hang up about the safety and concerns of those who can't think past the ass of the girl walking in front of them, you refuse to enjoy it for what it is. That my friend is the ultimate in hubris."

For the first time since he had first appeared on the bridge of the Enterprise, Bowie struck a nerve. "Okay Dr. Freud, if what you say is true, that makes me no better than the elite who feel it is their birthright to do the same. Just because I disagree with their methods, what makes you think the outcome would be any different because we are the ones running the show?"

"For the same reason I know that if you don't try, you will prove correct those who are attempting to eradicate humanity from existence – nothing more, nothing less."

This got Sean's attention. "Benevolent leadership from the end of a gun is still despotism, no matter how you spin it. Even if we do manage to succeed, absolute power corrupts absolutely. On the outside, one hundred years after we are dead, it's back to the same old same old, except this time armed with technology five hundred years ahead of its time."

Bowie gave Sean a look as if to say, *I know something you don't.* "Oh ye of little faith. This is a brave new world I am talking about. As much as I would like to share more about it, I will only say this. Tony, Renée, Alicia, Rebecca, and you are all that matters in the grand scheme of things in the here and now. You would be best served if you began to think in those terms."

"What does this make the other 10,000 plus sailors, cannon fodder?"

Bowie flashed a tired smile of acknowledgment and explained. "Let's just say the elements necessary to this particular situation does not call for an overabundance of concern for their wellbeing, as is true to those you destroyed in that Nazi task force. Do not mistake this to mean there is no value to their life force, just not in the here and now."

Sean exploded. "What kind of existential claptrap is that?"

"Now who is being disingenuous?" Bowie wagged his finger at Sean again. "I don't care how altruistic you appear to be, you and every other human still share the same strands of humanity as Stalin, Hitler, Attila the Hun, and every other sadistic maniac throughout the ages. You only reign in these psychopathic tendencies and insist on a different outcome. All one needs to do is track the ridiculous nature of your 20 year dance with your wife to see how hard you fight against your own self-interests."

This version of a more introspective Bowie continued his observations. "Then there is Tony, the one who is willing to go on the record unfiltered and full tilt politically incorrect. Now tell me Admiral, how do you feel about the parasitic propensity of the human race's ignorant rush to denude every resource on the planet? Where exactly is that utopian reality where every living thing is sacred?"

Now Bowie put his face close to Sean's to drive home his final point. "Because let me tell you, I have seen a million times more than you, the brutality of your species that is every bit as vicious as your understanding of Tyrannosaurus Rex. You just come in a smaller package, but then again so do the weapons of destruction you carry right here on this ship of war."

Now it was Sean's turn to smile. "Regardless of these truths you so eloquently point out, it appears you share the same maddening reality as we do, and that must be why you and your puppet masters have overturned time and space to create this drama.

"On the other hand, if it is you alone who has run out of patience, and you are the one who feels it is time to reset, clean the slate, flush us down the toilet, and start over, then all of this is strictly for your enjoyment. Maybe you're ready to try out some new toys with, oh, I don't know, creatures made out of snow instead of carbon."

Sean's sarcasm elicited a laugh from Bowie. "No wonder you didn't climb to your rightful place in the hierarchy. We have to do this more often, just the two of us. Anyway, we definitely got off the beaten track there. So what happens when you get to the Vatican and Captain Daily arrives at Greenwich Palace in London?"

It was Sean's turn to shrug as if to say *I know something you don't*. "And it is a wonder at all that the genius you decided to impersonate had a heart attack, because frankly, it is difficult to believe you have a heart." Sean began to walk away, not waiting for Bowie's usual fadeout, and over his shoulder sang a familiar song. "Time takes a cigarette, and puts it to your mouth," as he flicked his into the ocean.

"If that was only possible," Bowie shot back. "Oh, I almost forgot. Rebecca is going to want your attention in a few very short minutes."

Rebecca's head was flat on the only clear space on her desk, a bit of drool dripping off the side of her mouth. Like everybody else in the know, she expected violent exchanges of flesh-rending projectiles at any moment. Unlike anybody else, she also expected to hear from Carl. On the first, she was relieved, the second, in a state of rage.

Her eyes slowly opened, but it took a moment to get her bearings before she peeled her face off the desk, and focused her thoughts.

Forrest handed her the cup of coffee he had just poured for himself. "It's two in the morning, and so now you go right back to work? Why don't you take a break before you stroke out?"

"Thank you. I'll rest when I'm dead."

A warning chime turned their attention to Specter's monitor. The screen showed two distinct energy spikes, one, two hundred miles ahead of their current course, the other along the same course as Captain Daily's group. Before she could call the CIC, the klaxon call to General Quarters confirmed they were already aware of the same contacts.

"What now?" a weary Forrest asked as he slumped down into his chair.

Before she could answer, a summons came over the ship's speakers ordering Rebecca to the Admirals Ready Room. She directed a threat at Specter's monitor and muttered under her breath, "I'll deal with you later."

Five minutes later, she stood in front of Sean, Alicia, and Tony and Renée who both looked as if they had just rolled out of bed, which they had. "Based on the spike that announced the arrival of the Nazis, I can tell you this one is similar in nature, though split into exactly what you would expect if someone had knowledge of the distribution of our forces. It is a perfect counter to your strategy, Admiral."

Alicia, who was on the phone with the CIC, reported to Sean, "The task force is cloaked, Alpha Whiskey of Daily's group has confirmed the contacts, the recon air package has launched, and the Hampton has plotted a course to the threats."

"Give the go ahead to the Hampton." Sean turned to Rebecca. "Anything else to report on your end?"

"Nothing that pertains to us getting shot at again, or fantastical aberrations of great ego, or wayward absentee husbands able to mess with time and space, or for that matter a word from my son. I need a drink." Without asking, Rebecca walked over and poured a tumbler of Jack Daniels Single Barrel.

"I'll take that as a no," Sean replied a bit miffed.

Alicia walked over to Rebecca. "You mind pouring me one?" Alicia held out her glass. "You better be careful Rebecca, you are starting to sound like Tony, like my husband has lately. Such cynicism is bound to mess up the hip chick thing that you wear so well."

Tony shot Alicia a withering look. "At least I don't have any illusions of grandeur."

The phone rang again, and Alicia answered. "Thank you – hold please."

She then announced, "CIC reports multiple incoming bogeys."

Sean nodded, and rose to leave.

Rebecca stood up and grabbed her laptop. "Well back to the salt mines for me. Feel free to let me know if someone else decides to send another nuke our way."

Alicia hung up the phone, and watched the irritated scientist exit. "We have got to find a way to get that girl some rest. We should all be worried about her mental state."

"As much as I would like to agree with you, I don't see any way to let up with us under the constant threat of annihilation, and her as the only one who has the ability to maximize Specter's capabilities." Sean could feel the harshness in this assessment, but he had to reign in his feelings for the greater good.

Alicia sadly shook her head in agreement. "So, back to the CIC?"

Without a word, they filed out of the room to deal with the next crisis.

When they arrived, the atmosphere was tense with every station officer glued to their equipment. Sean took a seat near the CIC Officer on duty and after a briefing on the course and speed of the new contacts ordered, "Alter course 30 degrees starboard and maintain current speed. Maybe we can slip past them to the south."

"Yes Sir."

Meanwhile, three hundred miles southwest of Ireland, Captain Daily was in the middle of deciding his own command dilemma. The Princeton CIC reported surface contacts directly northeast on course to intercept. Captain Daily had few options without air cover, and burdened with two supply ships that were lucky to make 15 knots, stealth was their only hope. He ordered the Princeton CIC, "Change course to 25 degrees starboard, speed 15 knots, and maintain radio silence." He put the phone back and exhaled, "Rig for silent running."

For the next two hours, both elements of the task force slowly edged their way around their perspective obstructions.

—◆—

The speed that the barbarity took hold throughout the world filled Aaron with glee. Reports coming out of the NSA confirmed that China hadn't waited long after their ultimatum to launch cyberattacks that brought down both South Korean and Japanese Command and Control networks. Satellite information detailed and confirmed the missile launches that further decapitated these nations' ability to mount any coherent defense.

Aaron knew it would take only one more major nuclear exchange between the warring nations to send enough material into the atmosphere to reach the critical mass necessary to create a nuclear winter. In other words, a massive die-off of every living organism on the planet, the outcome he most desired – game over. Everything was happening exactly as he planned, so why did a nagging doubt about something he missed remain buried in the back of his consciousness?

In the cave in China, Sean Anthony and his hacker group were putting the final touches on the next surprise they had lined up for Aaron.

Phoenix got up from her chair, and gave out an exaggerated yawn as she stretched out her muscles like a cat. "Six straight hours in this chair is killing me. Why can't someone engineer an anti-gravity one that doesn't flatten your ass?"

Adonis couldn't resist an opportunity and jumped in. "There isn't an engineer on the planet that could fix that tiny white ass of yours."

Phoenix walked over to his workstation and lifted one of his hands as if to study. "Yeah, and if the size of a man's hand and feet signified the size of his other bits were true, that might explain why there is no woman in your life." To drive home the point she wiggled her little finger.

This got all the other hacker's attention, who now waited his response to her challenge of his manhood. He didn't disappoint.

"Or maybe the reason there isn't a woman in my life is because too many of them couldn't handle what I had to offer. But then again, what would someone with such a little ass know about that anyway?"

Phoenix talked as she glared at Adonis. "At least I come as advertised." She mocked him by grabbing her crouch, and putting her fingers a quarter inch apart." Everyone, including Sean Anthony burst into laughter at the dig.

"That's just cold, dawg."

Sean Anthony waited for the laughter in the cave to die down, and not wanting to see where they went from there, stepped in.

"That wraps up our work here. I figured we could all use a break, so grab your personal things, and let's go."

Once the group was prepared to leave, the green mist swirled.

As Aaron watched the information streaming real-time into the White House Situation Room, at first it didn't register that the latest missile launches out of China, which were targeted to hit Japan, began to fall off the monitors into the South China Sea. It wasn't until the Chief of Staff of the Air Force yelled out from across the White House Situation Room that Aaron's attention focused on the commotion that had suddenly erupted. "What's the problem, General Favors?"

"It looks like the systems the Chinese use to track their missiles have gone dark. Apparently they lost all of their uplinks." He picked up the phone as he talked and asked the other end, "You getting this? Do you know where the attack is originating?" After a moment of silence, he turned his attention back to Aaron. "You better inform the President to get down here pronto."

"Inform the President of what?" Aaron demanded.

"The NSA reports that not only have the Chinese lost control of their communications, their currency is under attack, and if you can believe it, the cyberattacks originated from right here in the States."

As if on cue, the White House Situation Room went dark until emergency generators came online seconds later. Though the lights came back on, the computer monitors remained dark, resisting the frantic subordinates' feverish attempts to re-establish contact with the outside world.

Aaron's rage grew as he starred at the room full of the nation's top military leadership who appeared completely impotent, and could offer little in the way of help. Then the final insult occurred when all the monitors came back online playing the same video. "Beelzebub has a devil put aside for me, for me, for me!"

Aaron laughed at Sean Anthony's choice of tunes. "Very funny.

Could someone please shut that down?"

Despite the efforts to yank all the plugs, Queen's Bohemian Rhapsody continued to play. "You should have been in pictures, Sean Anthony. Bravo."

Twenty minutes later back in the Oval Office, Aaron stood in front of President Harrison's desk, and he could see she was only moments away from a complete breakdown. In one hand, she held a stack of communiques, the other the phone. "Yes, we are aware the Chinese refused to comply with the United Nations resolution condemning their unprovoked attack on your nation Mr. President. No, our hands are full with our own problems. No, I haven't had the chance... If you could stop interrupt...," and that was it. President Susan Harrison lost it. "Listen asshole. I don't give a rat's ass about China right now, or for that matter anyone else. As far as..."

Aaron put his finger on the desk phone, disconnecting the call. "I think that is enough for now."

President Harrison slammed the phone down. "Do you? Considering almost every facet of communications, transportation, shipping, and most importantly, the nation's power grid has cascaded into failure. The White House is operating on emergency generators, and most of our secured communication connections to the outside world are down.

"The NSA, CIA, FBI, and just about every other damn acronym, are offline. Do you have a plan for this massive cluster fuck, Aaron? I can't even reach General Leigh to see how much this has impacted our military control of the cities."

Harrison was in a state of hysteria, so Aaron did the only thing that would make the situation more manageable for him. He pulled out a small caliber revolver from his coat pocket and fired a bullet between the eyes of the President. The bullet smashed through her forehead, and before it could exit the back of her head and slam into the bulletproof glass behind her, Aaron had turned to head back to his office.

The soundproofing in the Oval Office kept those outside from hearing the gunshot. Twenty minutes passed before Sarah Whineglaus found the bloody corpse and sounded the alarm, but outside of the President's immediate Secret Service detachment, the news had to travel by word of mouth. Shortly after her demise, the last of the White House elaborate communication systems had gone dark.

In the ensuing chaos, Aaron acted quickly. Not only was killing the President premature, in committing this direct intervention he opened the door for Sean Anthony to take the gloves off. However, this suited Aaron just fine. His action had freed him from decades of enforced restraint, which allowed his pent up rage to explode in a new orgy of bloodlust.

Phoenix and Sean Anthony found themselves standing in a hut with bamboo walls and a thatched roof.

Phoenix was not impressed. "What are we, Swiss Family Robinson now?" She looked around to see no one else from the cave arrived with them. "Where are the others?"

"Welcome to paradise on one of the over 1,000 islands of Polynesia, and the others are down on one of the most beautiful beaches you have ever seen. You like?"

Phoenix looked puzzled as she looked around the empty hut. "I hate. Not a computer in sight, and not even an outlet to plug one in if you had one. What's this about?"

"We disrupted cyber space throughout the globe, remember? Besides with Aaron out of control, I figured it would be wise to get as far off the grid as possible, so why not paradise? For now, the fewer people we have around us the better."

"How will we keep track of anything holed up here in a thatched hut?" Phoenix felt a growing sense of disorientation. This was the first time since she was four that she found herself disconnected from technology, and it was making her nervous.

"You're not thinking kiddo. What good would it do for us to have our workstations and servers when there is nothing left to access? Besides, you can click into almost any situation on the planet through your lineage."

Sean Anthony tried to get Phoenix to focus on the here and now. He walked over to the window, and pointed to the rest of their team. "Why don't you join the others and try to enjoy yourself while we're here. In fact, if you do you'll find a spread fit for a king, prepared by Queen Elizabeth's head chef."

Phoenix looked out to see the rest of the hacker team on the beach enjoying what looked like a royal banquet. She also realized she was starving. "What are we waiting for?"

Vice President Simon Fredericks opened the cigar box and pulled out one of his favorite Honduran Robusto cigars, which he immediately cut the tip and picked up the torch to light. "You know that with all the uncertainty in Washington at the moment, I think it would be a good time to take a little goodwill trip down to South America." Simon put the torch to the cigar and took several quick hits to distribute the burn evenly. "Did you hear what I said Elizabeth?"

"Elizabeth can't talk right now. It seems someone slashed her throat so deeply, it separated her vocal cords."

Stunned by the sound of Aaron's voice, the Vice President spun around to see his wife of thirty-three years hunched over, blood pouring from her neck.

Aaron sat calmly next to her, as he ran his fingers along the edge of the blood soaked knife he had used to slit her throat. "It's the simple things in life that give the most pleasure, don't you think?"

He watched as the blood drained from Simon's face, too stunned to move or speak. Then the mechanism in his brain kicked in that informed him now would be the time to run away as fast as the surge of adrenaline would allow. Unfortunately, two steps was one too many to take as the knife Aaron threw buried itself deeply into the center of his neck. He fell forward grasping at the hilt in an attempt to pull it out.

Before he could succeed, Aaron stood over his thrashing body and with his left foot stomped the knife so hard it drove right through the front of his neck and pinned the man to the floor. Aaron grabbed the nearest chair, picked up the still lit cigar off the floor, and spent the next ten minutes smoking it as he watched Simon die a slow painful death. "Oh well. Break time is over. So many people to kill – so little time. What's a poor boy supposed to do?"

Over the course of the next two hours, Aaron made similar visits to butcher in the brutal manner he had spent years dreaming about, the Speaker of the House, President Pro Tempore of the Senate, the Secretary of State, and all the other government leaders who could lay claim to the presidency.

In the home of his last victim, he took a leisurely shower to wash the blood off before picking out a tailor-made suit to wear. Moments later, he sat in his office reliving each kill as he finished the former Vice President's cigar.

While Aaron went on his rampage in the nation's capital, the individual military unit Commanders who enforced the edicts of martial law found themselves cut off from their Commander in Chief, the Pentagon, and GCCS [Department of Defense joint Global Command and Control System].

With so many of the Army's units supplemented with National Guard units whose ties with the local populations went back generations, conversations turned to the hardships these families and friends faced. For the first time since the President had ordered martial law, individual soldiers began to question why citizens from cities such as Kansas City could possibly pose a threat to the country.

With all civilian internet and phone networks also down, the green first lieutenants on the front line, now left on their own to command those enforcing the curfews, struggled with their moral obligations and began to allow minor breaches. This led to something quite remarkable for the times. People began to come out of their homes and talk face to face with others in their communities. Without the glow emanating from their numerous social media devices, it was like witnessing a zombie movie in reverse.

———◆———

Rebecca's adrenaline surged when Specter's monitor began to flash red. The screen then split into numerous windows showing contacts that popped up throughout the task force. Rebecca rapidly disseminated the information to discover this was a completely different threat. She picked up the phone and called the CIC. "We have intruders throughout the task force."

Sean, Alicia, and Tony were still in the CIC when Rebecca reported the power spikes on every one of the warships. Oddly, to Sean none of these contacts showed up on the supply ships or in any of the spaces taken up by Specter's systems. "General Quarters, notify the Marines stationed in the reactor, armaments, and propulsion compartments that deadly force is authorized." To Rebecca, who had waited on the phone, he ordered, "Stay put. I have sent an additional detachment of Marines to your location. Can you transfer the contacts directly to each of the ships?"

"Already done Admiral. I was also able to upload the info directly to each ship's Marine Commander, but I am confused Specter wasn't their target. You want to cripple us, knock out Specter."

"We will worry about that anomaly after we clear the ships. Out."

Always packing his side arm, Tony decided he wasn't going to sit it out. "I'm going to join the Marines at the reactors."

Sean was about to countermand the order when Alicia grabbed

his arm. "Let him go. We need his eyes."

Sean threw Tony a radio. "Keep us informed."

It didn't take long before Tony found himself in the middle of it. As he climbed down to the reactor level, a bullet ricocheted off the bulkhead in front of him. He crouched down and looked around the corner to see two Marines down, and another two returning fire against assailants he couldn't see from his current position. He motioned his intent to the other Marines after running the ship's schematics through his mind. He climbed back up the stairs, turned in the opposite direction, ran through five bulkheads, climbed down two flights of stairs, ran across two bulkheads back the other way, and looked up the next set of stairs. With no one visible, he slowly climbed up and raised his head through the opening. Satisfied, he rushed the last three steps onto the deck. He took out four assailants with his side arm who were guarding the entrance into the reactor spaces, and yelled out, "Hostiles down, this is Captain Knox."

Slowly heads poked around the far corner, and when they saw Tony, they rushed to his side. One particularly giant of a man gave him a good thump on the chest.

"Good to see you again, Thorny." Tony rubbed where Commander Michael Thornton had struck him. "Shall we continue?"

Thorny motioned for his sapper to blow the door, which exploded inward moments later. Commander Thornton led the way with Tony in trail as they rushed in to find two men attaching explosives around the room. Caught in the conundrum between finishing arming the weapons or defending themselves, they lost the option for either as the SEALs and Tony ended their existence. Tony walked up to one of the bodies, and was not happy at the insignia stitched to the invaders shoulder.

Tony immediately contacted Sean, and gave him the all clear. "Six total, six down. We have four down, and two on the way to

Sickbay, one critical. What about the others?"

"Armaments are secured. Same six man teams, all down, but nothing from…"

At that moment, a large blast shook the massive ship, and Tony lost contact with Sean. He looked at Thorny and shouted, "Propulsion!"

They could feel the ship's speed bleed off as they ran further aft. When they were within 100 yards of their target, thick smoke blocked their path. Tony grabbed Thorny. "Find out what you can, and if you can't re-establish radio contact, set up a relay to CIC, which is where I am heading. I'll keep trying to…"

At that moment, Sean came back on the radio. "Tony you copy?"

"Right here. From where I am and the amount of smoke, it looks like they blew one of our center shafts."

Emergency fire teams arrived and began to add their equipment to the automatic systems that supplied a steady stream of fire suppressant to the smoke filled corridor. "I'm heading back. Commander Thornton is here, and will keep us informed. Any news from the rest of the fleet?"

"Apparently, thirty percent seems to be the ratio." Sean hesitated for a moment.

Alicia took the phone. "They blew a pretty big hole in us Tony. Damage reports are still coming in, but we have casualties on every warship, and we have no idea what's going on aboard the Hampton with her being out of radio contact."

Tony took in the news, and looked at the jacket in his hand. "The insignia on one of the attacker's uniform was a Crescent moon. It looks like another reality with the Jihadists in charge has checked in." The jacket fell from his hand and hit the deck as he walked away.

The CIC Officer handed Alicia the latest casualty figures, which she quickly read through. "These numbers bring our estimated losses to over 350 KIA, 876 injured, and still haven't heard from the Hampton. Based on combatant losses and the lack of any terrorist survivors, we can safely assume this was a suicide attack." Alicia went silent as she struggled to continue. "And what if we over estimated their naval capabilities, and should have attacked directly?"

Sean agreed. "Yes, I was thinking the same thing, only if they can't see us cloaked, how did they manage to slip over 100 terrorists on board our ships?"

"You do realize the whole idea of using an *American* naval task force commanded by *Americans* is for you to respond as *Americans*. Of course they managed to sneak sappers onto your ships."

Bowie was back, or by the look of their new surroundings, they were back at Tony's house in Cuba. "If you are not willing to bring the fight to them, they will always bring the fight to you. If we wanted clever bastards who were adverse to violence, we would have brought the French in your place."

This was an opportune time for Tony to enter the room. Though he expected to be entering the corridor after stepping through the door from the CIC, instead he found himself back in his home hearing Bowie admonishing Sean's tactics. "Shit!"

Bowie wasn't through. "This is your plan? Hide and Seek?" I thought we were long past the peace, love, and drugs of the 60s. Where have all the Rebels gone?"

His antics sent Alicia into a rage. "How dare you question our attempt to avoid contact with an unknown force, an unknown that is probably as confused as us about why they are here. For all we know they want a fight with us less than we want with them."

"Such a silly girl. Here you have centuries of data proving the violent nature of nations, and you think they could be innocents? But of course, clouds are made of cotton candy, unicorns are real, and if you wish hard enough, true love always wins in the end."

Alicia stepped over to go face-to-face with Bowie. "So your

solution is for the good guys to win the day is by proving we can succeed by being more brutal than the bad guys?"

Bowie shrugged his shoulders. "Well, duh. How else did you think it works? Those weren't pamphlets espousing the wonder of Jesus the Allies were dropping over Berlin in WWII. As much as I wish you would take my word for it, your job is to wipe out evil as I see it, and trust that my intentions are pure."

Bowie's statement got Sean, Alicia, and Tony to stop and stare at each other in amazement for a moment, before they all broke into laughter. Alicia was first to gain control. "Trust you? You possess supernatural abilities that allow you to move us around as marionettes, and you think we would trust you to decide what is in our best interests?"

Still in Bowie's face, Alicia wasn't through. "On top of that, seeing what you are capable of, for all we know, it is more than likely your kind is responsible for the Hell on Earth our world is perpetually in. And now, you are branching out and creating whole new realities to muck up. You and your kind seem to take great pleasure in the disintegration of the world you yanked us out of. You have a reality that is stable, one coming apart at the seams, and the one we now inhabit where a couple of supernatural beings impersonating icons play with lives like spoiled children who enjoy torturing small animals. David Bowie you are not."

"And what makes you think what happens in one reality does not impact another, or for that matter, thousands of others." Franklin entered from the kitchen, wiping his hands on a towel; an apron with *Kiss the Chef* emblazoned across the front adorned his girth. "Who is to say the pot roast I have in the oven is not changing the future course of an entire universe. None of us in this room can be sure of anything other than we are all victims of what we don't know."

At that moment, the bathroom door opened and a surprised Renée joined them. She had expected the corridor outside of the

Admirals Ready Room. "I'll never get used to this." Then, without skipping a beat, asked the gathering, "So, what did I miss?"

"The usual, honey," Tony replied. "You know, one diva pissed off for not getting what he thinks he wants, the other reminding us that all of creation is at stake. Cup of coffee anyone?"

Though Sean, consumed with what might be still threatening his command, didn't feel like taking on Tony's flippant attitude, his efforts so far were not having the right effect. "So we act aggressively, people die, we act passively people die, and if we do nothing at all, people die, and somewhere out there one of my former Commanders is hovering over all of it like The Watcher."

Alicia joined in. "Don't forget his and Rebecca's son, Sean Anthony, who neither you nor I have had the pleasure of meeting."

"How about if I am really dead, never really died, or will die if you all leave?"

"Good, point Renée. So exactly how does our situation tie into your two little maniacs' machinations?" Sean looked mockingly around the room. "Speaking of Rebecca, shouldn't she have her say, because you have to know she can get worked up when secrets are kept from her?"

Though Bowie looked as if he would like nothing better than end all of their lives on the spot, Franklin maintained his usual charm. "Honestly, dinner is getting cold, and if I didn't know better we might have a chance of ironing out our differences over a nice glass of port and a hot meal." He motioned for everyone to follow, as he walked toward the dining room and added over his shoulder. "In regards to Rebecca, she is a little busy right now. Come, come."

Sean was about to argue, but Alicia stopped him with a finger to her lips. "After dinner lover. I'm sure nothing is happening, or for that matter if time is even moving for our ships and crews."

Back in Specter's operations center aboard the Enterprise, Rebecca knew how Scottie from Star Trek felt as she fielded a barrage of questions from the different engineers in the task force as she coordinated the upgrades to Specter's operating systems and equipment. Though the terrorists didn't attack Specter directly, there were a myriad of issues created by external damages that affected the interfaces between the individual ships and Specter's main control system on the Enterprise. For every answer she gave to questions from her new team of engineers, she created ten news ones for them to ask.

"That isn't what I said. In fact, it is exactly the opposite of what I asked from you. When I tell you to decouple the grid from the operating system before you install the transducers, I didn't think there was any way that you would do it with the power still on. Now we have to use one of our last spare transducers to replace the one you blew up."

She had more to say to the chagrined engineer aboard the John Paul Jones, but right in the middle of her dressing him down, a voice entered her consciousness. "You do know this isn't a good time."

"It never is."

One minute Rebecca was on a call with the engineer on the John Paul Jones, the next she was face to face with a young, pretty girl in what appeared to be a hut that looked like it belonged in some 1960s movie set on a Polynesian island. Looking out the window to the beach below, she could make out several young teenagers and one hulking black man in his thirties who stood out while lying on the whitest sand she had ever seen. The hut, the white sand, and the aquamarine colored ocean water made the whole scene look like a travel agency brochure.

Looking back at her host, something was strangely familiar about the child, and without skipping a beat Rebecca asked, "Where do I know you from? Did you do work for Comstock Technologies while we were developing Specter?"

Phoenix laughed at the thought of a Black Hat like her ever working for the enemy, but then again her mother-in-law would know that about her, which made her wonder, "Why was Rebecca acting like she had never seen me before?"

With the knowledge that this was either by Carl's design or some trick of Aaron's, Phoenix decided to go along with it until she knew more. "Never been inside Comstock, and since you are almost old enough to be my mother, and the only way we could have met was if you had a passion for washed up rocker concerts."

She reached out her hand in greeting. "Then again if you're a regular visitor in the Dark Cloud, you would know me by the handle of Phoenix."

Rebecca took her hand. "Dr. Rebecca Cutler, and as much as I am a fan of 60s Rock, most of them were broken up or dead by the time I was *old* enough."

Rebecca scanned the hut and noticed there wasn't a single electronic device to be seen. "This looks more like a place you would find James Gardner and Doris Day than a crash pad for kids. Where are the iPhones, tablets, and laptops no self-respecting young adult would be caught dead without?"

"I don't know. Maybe we wanted to see how our elders communicated with rotary dial telephones, and a shout out the window to Miss Crabtree next door for social media." Though Phoenix enjoyed messing with her mother-in-law, she also subtly edged her way toward the kitchen looking for a convenient weapon to pick up in case it wasn't her.

Rebecca was getting a little testy at why she now stood in front of this cynical woman-child, and she didn't have any trouble picking up Phoenix's intentions. "Really? You think I am a threat?" Rebecca then looked up to nowhere special and yelled out, "Carl, this is getting old. Could you please get your ass in here?"

That was the Rebecca Phoenix remembered. "Relax. We're all a little uptight around here, what with everyone trying to kill us and all."

Before Rebecca could respond, Adonis walked through the front door. "Why aren't you down on the beach with the rest of…?" It was then that he saw Rebecca. After a moment to get over the surprise of seeing a stranger in the hut, he smiled. "It's about time he brought someone in here that didn't make me feel like a pedophile." Adonis towered over Rebecca as he walked over and offered his hand. "So what's your skillset beautiful?"

A voice from behind him announced, "Her skillset, Mr. Mean and Nasty, is mother, as in my mother."

Adonis quickly jumped back at the sound of Sean Anthony's voice. "Sorry dude; my bad." Though embarrassed at flirting with anyone's mother, Adonis quickly decided some snacks would go well with what might come next and headed to the kitchen.

"Hello mother." Sean Anthony quickly found himself wrapped up in a hug, the kind that felt like it would never end. After several failed attempts to disengage from his mother without success, he pleaded to her. "Not in front of the children, mom."

With a laugh, Rebecca finally released her grasp on him. "So what exactly are you doing in a Polynesian hut with a bunch of obvious delinquents? What's your father got you into this time?"

"Nothing we can't handle." Phoenix stated this as a given.

Rebecca glared at Phoenix. "And who is this little bundle of joy?"

Sean Anthony moved quickly to put himself between the two women. "My apologies. Rebecca Eddington, this is Phoenix, and she is an important member of my team. Phoenix, it would serve all of us better if you lost the attitude." Sean Anthony stopped for a second, thinking about what he just said. "By the way, why do you have an attitude?"

"I was surprised that's all. For all I knew she could have been one of Aaron's minions." Then under her breath, she added, "And still could be."

Rebecca took in her son's reaction to Phoenix, and smiled. "So how long have you two been together? Any kids?" Then her son's appearance struck Rebecca hard and her heart broke. "How could I have missed so much of your life?" That she was absent as he made the transition from boy to man slammed her in the gut so hard Rebecca buried her face in his chest. "How could Carl let me miss so much?"

"If you could see it from dad's perspective, you would realize it isn't such a big deal."

Wrong answer. "How dare you say that to me? The last time I saw you, you were all of 6 years old, and now here you are, what now fifteen, twenty years older? Your father has gotten away with leaving me in the dark about what you two are up to, but I will not take that from my son."

Returning from the kitchen with a hand full of cookies, Adonis plopped down on the couch. "Let me tell you, man. If I tried laying that shit on my mother, I don't care how old I was, I wouldn't be sitting down for a week."

"At least your mother got to watch you grow up," Rebecca rebuked.

"Ouch," Adonis answered, as he winced in faux pain.

Phoenix was about to join in, but the look on Sean Anthony's face stopped her cold. Instead, she walked over to Adonis and reached out her hand. "Why don't we join everyone on the beach and give them some privacy."

"And miss this?" Before he could continue, the look on both Sean Anthony and Phoenix's face convinced him it was time to go. It was nice meeting you Mama E. Feel free to drop by any time." With a final push from Phoenix, he disappeared out the door.

Now alone with her son, Rebecca let it all out. "So, you can share what you're doing with a bunch of kids, but your fully grown up mother with two PhDs in physics and computer engineering is left in the dark?"

"Now you're being silly. Besides dad wasn't the only one who thought it would be a bad idea if you knew too much about what we are trying to do."

"And who would that be?"

Sean Anthony shrugged his shoulders, and thought, "What the hell, I can't win either way," he thought before answering. "That would be you, and if you want to know why, you had better ask dad because there is no way in hell that I am going to get in the middle of that."

This news brought Rebecca to a standstill. "Me? Why would I agree to that? You know how I hate secrets."

"Surprised me as well, when dad told me."

Rebecca slowly made her way to the couch and sat down. Her mind was spinning at a million miles a second going over all the events that led her to this moment. Sean Anthony knew better than interrupt her thought process.

After ten minutes of silence, her emotional half came to terms with the analytical half. "So what exactly do you hope to accomplish with all of this?" Rebecca's hands opened up as she raised them above her head as a gesture to mock the primitive state of Sean Anthony's operations.

The tone of Rebecca's voice enabled Sean Anthony to relax. "Dad thought it would be the only time we could get some rest, so what better place for a bunch of kids to relax than on a beach. Why don't we go down and join them? The reason you are here is to enjoy a little time with me. It would be a shame to waste the opportunity."

For the first time since she arrived, Rebecca smiled. "I can't think of anything that could be better." She wrapped her arm around his waist as they left the hut.

———⊰⊱———

Darius [Carl Eddington] stood on a high bluff overlooking the Northern Pacific admiring the way the wind gusts created a swirling mass of white caps on the storm-tossed sea below. "For all the damages humanity has inflicted upon this magnificent planet, there were still vast untamed wildness areas unlike any other in this part of the Galaxy. A billion years of evolution is how the educated Darwinian thinkers of humanity choose to view its direct timeline, but I know better. Over half that time I have witnessed, and in many cases helped to shape the life forms that have lived and decayed to dust on it.

"From the first single-celled life form to the moment life crawled out of the sea, ninety-nine percent of all life on this planet was created solely to prepare the planet for what was to come. Seven hundred million years of evolution led to the planet's longest existing tenants, the dinosaurs, who then roamed the Earth for over two hundred fifty million years. Now that was an impressive breeding program," Darius said to his companion. "And that was utilizing only one percent of what we endowed on humanity."

"Or you might say one giant ego trip to prove the power of an individual who got bored with life in his little secluded corner of the Milky Way." Cromulus [Jesus] stood next to Darius enjoying the view. "I only got involved because it sounded like fun to watch a few simians acting like us for a couple of hundred thousand years, only nothing ever evolved, even after they were shown the way forward millions of times over."

Darius turned to face him. "Only because Durius used a million different ways to stifle any change, or I should say changes for the better. She certainly made sure they always evolved more efficient ways of killing each other."

For this visit, Cromulus eschewed his usual Jesus robes and sandals in favor of a Jimmy Buffet concert shirt and shorts, and of course, he was sipping on a margarita. "Personally speaking, I have to admit the whole idea of adding evil to the mix was fun for a while. I especially enjoyed how dropping in the simple idea that gold was something to kill for made them all go crazy. It was one thing to watch the human's battle over resources, but introducing greed in the form of a shiny rock exposed a major flaw in what you tried to create. You've got to give Durius credit for that."

Darius wasn't having any of that as he produced his own

margarita. "Give her credit? I don't think so. You are conveniently forgetting that all six of us knew before agreeing to imprint them with some of our DNA that their primitive instincts would be a problem that would take thousands of generations to weed out."

"Too bad for you that we can only travel a time line that has already played out, or you could have foreseen your little dalliance would have induced her reactions," Cromulus countered.

"You take the good with the bad," Darius sighed. "It isn't like I didn't know the flaw existed when I picked the primitive humans. They were the only creature with the necessary anatomy and a brain developed enough to integrate our genes."

Cromulus took another sip of his margarita. "Again, too bad for you the few who did evolve into something special were too sparse in number to do you any good. But then again we both know the only reason Durius let some of them achieve recognition was to drive you crazy with what could have been."

Darius shook his head in agreement before he shifted some of the blame to Cromulus. "Even that wouldn't be so bad if you hadn't created monotheism. Once *your* Christian God told them that their primary purpose in life was to procreate and that life was a matter of faith, all reason went out the door."

"At the time you and Durius were in agreement, so when she played up what a great idea it was, how would I know she had ulterior motives?" Cromulus said in defense.

"Right *you* didn't know," Darius sneered. "The reason I finally put my plan into action was because the church put da Vinci under house arrest for reporting what he could see with his own eyes to be true. And could you please explain to me why it made any difference to the Roman Catholic Church if the Sun circled the Earth or the Earth circled the Sun?"

Cromulus countered Darius's question with a question. "If you can explain to me how a society could live in relative harmony where anyone could worship the god of their choice, take for example the

Greeks, Romans, and other societies who lived with polytheism, and yet, when given only one to worship, it turns everyone into raging psychopaths. However, I have to admit that I still don't understand how one simple bad idea can create so much brutality, death, and destruction; a true stroke of genius on her part."

Cromulus raised his glass. "To the devious genius of Durius."

Sadly, once again Darius had to agree. "I never said she was stupid."

"So, *Darius*, was Rebecca worth all of this trouble?"

"Well I don't know, *Cromulus*, was Mary Magdalene worth it to you? I recall you sharing a good part of your time over the last two thousand years with her many incarnations. You can't tell me you don't have any skin in the game."

Cromulus shook his head no. "You forget one simple fact Sherlock. I don't have an ex-wife like you have with Durius. When I decide to mix it up with the natives, I don't have anyone looking over my shoulder ready to blast me when I do."

Darius took a long sip of his margarita before he changed the subject. "I find it ironic that the one who has been the messenger to billions of our creations is the last one of us who would take the time to create anything of his own."

Cromulus laughed. "That's because you have no idea how much fun it is to be able to pop in and out of everyone else's work. No one at our level knows more about what drives so many of us to imprint the universe with pieces of ourselves than me. So when you question why it was so easy for Durius to get your pets to procreate themselves to near extinction, look to that part of you in them for your answer."

"Yeah, like that's never gotten you into trouble before," Darius sneered. "Why was it exactly that Durius made a whore out of *your* human wife? Oh, I remember, it's because you refused to return after Durius turned the name of Jesus into an instrument of death."

"I always felt that you enjoyed your role as Messiah a little too much," Darius added with a smile. "Personally speaking, my favorite of your prophet incarnations is Buddha." Darius raised his refilled glass. "Here's to the Jolly Buddha."

Cromulus laughed as they clinked their glasses together. "Buddha was fun, but you should have spent more time with John the Baptist. Now he was a prophet who could fill an amphitheater. I swear he could hypnotize you into believing he was the second coming. I always say, learn from the best."

They both took a moment of silence to watch the Sun set over the horizon, clicking their glasses together when it disappeared.

Cromulus spoke, ending the moment. "It is too bad that it all has to end this way. I was looking forward to eventually finishing my roles. Darius, could you imagine the turmoil I would have created the first time modern humans saw me walking on water?"

"Hah," Darius laughed. "In this day and age, they would have thought you learned the trick from David Copperfield. You would have had to rain gold from the sky to get their attention, and even then Congress would have held up the bill declaring it a true miracle in committee because some idiot asshole from Alabama attached a rider banning abortions."

Cromulus looked at Darius in amazement "And you want to save them, why?"

"Who said anything about saving them?" Darius shook his head no. "I want to salvage those who do see life for what it can be even if their sacrifices take a lifetime to move the needle even a micron in the right direction. They are the ones who are worth giving the reward of full disclosure to. Not the millions who spend their lives trying to climb over each other to see who can out consume who, or the ones whose perverted religion tells them to kill in the name of their god for righteousness sake."

"Oh Darius, you forget that it is the offspring of those pure of heart you defend so ardently who are the worst offenders when allowed to set the rules. I think the main thing Durius accomplished was to distract you from seeing the reality of what you created. After twenty-seven thousand years you still only have a one in a billion chance the next child born carries enough of our genes to overcome its primitive ones.

"I have a better idea. Rather than continue this charade, why not yank Rebecca out of this mess, and keep her as a souvenir for better days?"

Darius ignored the souvenirs dig. "Oh ye of little faith."

He smiled as he picked up a rock and threw it over the cliff and watched it disappear into the ocean mist. "You don't see me sweating, do you?"

"Well maybe you should." Cromulus answered as he too picked up a rock and threw it into the ocean mist below. "However, I will grant you that your offspring and his compatriots are putting on a much better show than I thought them capable of. I especially liked your gambit with the reality shifting, though it does seem you risked so much for so little gain. And your time with the Pope – that was priceless. First time I actually rooted for Aaron."

Cromulus then became serious. "However, Darius, there is something I think you may not have thought all the way through, and, knowing you better than most, that says something."

"Let me guess," Darius interjected. "That I may be acting a little bit reckless with all of these moving pieces, and should tone it down before other prying eyes might be drawn to the conflict?"

Cromulus could hear in the tone of Darius's voice that his warning would go unheeded. "Well there is that, but not what I had in mind. What concerns me is it seems both you and Durius are enjoying all of this more than either of you would care to admit. It's almost as if all of this hatred you're throwing back and forth only serves to escalate the game."

"Why Cromulus, are you analyzing my motives?"

"Only pointing out the obvious that it is in our blood to prove our intellect any chance we get, and what better way to do that than when under threat. Let's face it, since the day you first bedded your fair Rebecca, you haven't exactly been much fun to hang around with, especially after Durius found out."

"Ergo the final solution – duh." Darius threw his arms around his companion. "Trust me dear friend, I've got this."

Cromulus grabbed Darius's shoulders as he pulled away, and looked him in the eye. "The only thing Durius will accept is the complete annihilation of the one who she feels led you into betrayal. You may not have had to face that particular insult in your long and illustrious life, but believe me when I say even our supposed superiority still crumbles in the face of that kind of emotional betrayal."

"You should talk. Since Mary Magdalene turned your head and you took her back to your queer little world, I am the only friend you still have. After you left, not only did I make your Jesus the biggest name since Moses, but over one-third of the human population now uses your name as an excuse to commit almost every atrocity."

Darius laughed as Cromulus morphed his appearance into the Western society norm for Jesus: the beatific face, a long blonde beard, flowing white robes, and topped off with a brightly shimmering gold halo above his head. "Too much?"

Darius couldn't resist. "One man's savior is another man's devil."

Cromulus turned to walk toward the water for show, but stopped short, and returned to put his hand on Darius's shoulder. "You do know that if these reality shifts continue it's not only Durius you have to worry about. Some of the others have been looking for something new to get in the middle of, and have noticed the breeches of protocol you and Durius have committed. So far I have managed to neuter their interest, which wasn't that difficult because, let's get real no one gives a damn if humans disappear."

Now Darius was suspicious. "So what did you promise in return?"

"Oh yeah, the reason for my visit," Cromulus remembered. "No more cross reality intercourse. You stay away from both Rebecca and Sean Anthony. They succeed on their own, or game over."

"I will if Durius does the same. If she stops interfering with Rebecca and her friends in the 1492 reality, I will leave Sean Anthony to defeat Aaron on his own in the 2018 reality."

"Deal. I'll go inform the others."

With this agreement, Cromulus disappeared leaving Darius alone once again, this time to mull over his feelings for Rebecca. He thought back to how the curiosity of the primitive humans decided their place in his creation, and how, with her raw genius, Rebecca was everything he had hoped for at this point in human evolution. Add to it the excitement of being a part of each new step forward and the awe that came from it was a feeling Darius had not experienced for millions of years. "Worth saving? Hell yes."

Five minutes into dinner at Tony's house in Cuba, the odd collection of guests had not spoken a word. Suddenly and without the familiar green mist to announce it, both Franklin and Bowie disappeared in a flash, replaced by the fully sainted version of Jesus in the Son of God mode, three feet off the floor and hands reaching out. With the voice of the Almighty, he proclaimed, "There will not be any further attacks made on you, your ships, or any other humans attached to your service by forces from outside of this reality. You have clear sailing to your chosen locations. Use your time wisely."

He landed on the ground with a thud, and reached for the pot roast, out of which he took a generous bite. "Nice, but could have used another ten minutes in the oven." Then he too vanished, leaving the four too stunned to react.

Tony couldn't resist. "Does that mean this is our last supper?"

Seconds later and now seated in the Admirals Ready Room, Sean immediately grabbed the phone and called down to Rebecca. "Is Specter still registering the enemy power spikes?"

Fresh from her return, Rebecca immediately shifted gears and looked at the monitor. "All indicators are clear of outside power projections. The sea is clear ahead, Admiral. How did you know?"

"Let's just say we had a visit from another historical figure, and by comparison, he put Bowie and Franklin on the D-list."

After going over the damage reports from the Enterprise group, Sean ordered Captain Daily, by way of the E2D Advanced Hawkeye on station to the north, to report on the severity of damages to to the northern group so he could decide if they should steer a new course to trail the Enterprise group into the Mediterranean for repairs.

Captain Daily quickly gave Sean his status report. "Outside of a few casualties, and minor damages to most of my command we were lucky. The only incidence of note occurred on the Shiloh when the sappers managed to gain access to the ship's navigation computers. Fortunately we obtained replacement parts from the Schwarzkopf, and Captain Jackson's crew has already made repairs."

"Thank you Mark," Sean acknowledged. "Same here, though we took more casualties. On the plus side, Captain Turner of the Hampton finally made contact and reported nothing out of the ordinary after being out contact. We are about ready to have a burial service on the flight deck of the Enterprise to honor the dead. As surreal as our lives currently are, the least we can do is to give our dead the proper homage they deserve."

"Amen to that, Admiral."

"Stay safe Mark."

Aaron was dealing with the aftermath of the previous night's bloodletting, and by comparison, alcohol hangovers had nothing on how bad he felt. He stumbled out of his bed in tony Georgetown, with a thousand recriminations burning through his mind.

By the time the Secret Service agents arrived with the body count from the night before, Aaron concluded there wasn't any point to continue the charade any longer. After all, now that he had shredded some of the most highly visible leaders in the world, Sean Anthony could now personally intercede. One of the few positive traits Aaron possessed was the ability to understand his own weaknesses. "I wouldn't be able last three minutes if I go up against my brother, but I can use his mind-sharing method to wreak havoc with his darlings."

The stunned Secret Service agents watched as Aaron disappeared in a green flash. After twelve hours of nonstop failure to protect those they had sworn to give their lives to, this final shock was more than the two of them were willing to bear. "So, *Ralphie Boy*, the cabin in British Columbia? I can have the family ready by the time you swing by."

His partner thought for only a moment before he decided, "British Columbia it is." Forty-eight hours later, the two families crossed the border to Vancouver, BC and dropped off the grid for good.

Aaron suddenly appeared in front of the surprised Prime Minister of Russia Sergei Romanov, the apparent Czar in waiting. "Yes, I think you will do nicely, though would you mind putting on a shirt?"

Sergei Romanov leaned back in his old world overstuffed bright red chair. The very décor of his office was a throwback to the days of empire, when the world trembled at the former might of the now extinct Soviet Union. Though his bloated sense of self-importance always knew that his destiny included a place in the annals of history, he never saw this coming.

At their earlier meeting, Aaron accessed Russia's nuclear launch codes, and the disposition of both China's and the United States' threat protocols. "I sense you are disappointed with my gift to you."

He glared at Aaron. "What good is any of this if I can't even get my Mercedes to start?"

Bat Shit Crazy

Aaron was certainly in no mood to listen to the despot whine. "Since you have been so busy enjoying your newfound powers, you forgot the tiny task I required from you in return."

Sergei threw Aaron a menacing look. "I will do as I wish, and maybe I will wish to comply." Then as he thrust his face forward to drive home his point, he concluded, "And then maybe not."

"Russians and all their strong arm drama. With the Chinese you get riddles, the Arabs a knife in the back or shrapnel out of a vest, and with the Russians, macho baboon muscle heads." Aaron didn't need to appear threatening and simply stated the obvious. "Then there is the simple manner of your ability to breath. You bought in when I visited you earlier, so now I own you."

Suddenly the strong-arm Russian Premier's eyes went wild as he realized he could not draw a breath. Both his mouth and nose were in place, but when he tried to suck in air, nothing happened. Sergei struggled to rise out of the chair but could only flail away to no effect as his face began to turn a nasty shade of blue, while Aaron calmly watched the terror on his face grow. This quickly turned into a desperate attempt to plead for mercy, but no words came out of a mouth without a set of lungs to propel his larynx into action.

Aaron waited until Sergei was moments from unconsciousness before he snapped his fingers.

Sergei collapsed on his desk as he gulped for air like a beached guppy.

"Now how about we continue with what I want, and then maybe I will allow you to keep your lungs?" Aaron nonchalantly walked over to the bottle of Vodka on the table, poured himself a glass, and downed it. "Da?"

Five minutes later when Sergei's face returned to its normal pallor, he tripped over himself to meet Aaron's demands. After he completed the necessary calls to issue his orders, Sergei informed Aaron, "It will take 10 days to position six divisions on the Latvian border."

Aaron smiled. "Now see, that wasn't so hard, was it? I don't care if it takes weeks to accomplish, as long as you keep the European Union tied up trying to figure out what your intentions are. Now for the part that is going to knock your socks off."

Aaron reached over and tapped the surprised Sergei on the forehead, and the tyrant fell into his history. He vaguely heard Aaron state, "Two can play at this game."

Tom Abernathy wasn't in the best of moods. The Assistant Secretary to the President wasn't used to being left out of the President's agenda, but since the former President's Chief of Staff effectively took over for the departed Susan Harrison, Tom was nothing more than a glorified gopher. This became the least of his worries when his mind suddenly lost the ability to form a coherent thought as Sergei brute forced his way into the frustrated assistant's consciousness. Even on the best of his days, Tom's mind was anything but firm, so there wasn't much of a struggle for Sergei to dominate the weaker man. He didn't waste any time as he walked over to Sarah Whineglaus after picking up Tom's ornate letter opener and stated with a threatening eastern European accent. "You know someone I need to talk to."

Phoenix was almost asleep when something began to tug at her consciousness. She wasn't sure if it was the start of another of the weird series of dreams she experienced every night since her awakening, or something different. So she let it ride for a moment, at least until she felt a sharp pain penetrate her neck. Phoenix jumped up and scanned the room to find no one else there, yet the pain only intensified. "Sean Anthony! I need you!"

In less than 30 seconds, Sean Anthony arrived on a dead run and violently threw aside the makeshift curtain to find Phoenix up against the wall, her neck stretched out as if an invisible force held something to her throat. He knew what had happened and quickly took control of the situation. "Try to calm down and tell me what you see."

Through clenched teeth and short breaths, Phoenix slowly managed to answer. "Sarah's assistant at the White House, Tom Abernathy has a knife to my – I mean her throat, but I feel it too!"

Sean Anthony again motioned for her to stay calm and asked in a calm voice, "Find out what he wants."

"Simple enough. You will remove the malware you used to attack Russia's communications systems, or I will slit your throat, and I will continue to slit every last one of your throats across the world until I find and slit yours."

Sean Anthony focused all of his attention on Phoenix, and in a low voice counseled, "Who else do you sense in proximity to Sarah? Maintain contact with Sarah, but reach out with your senses."

"I'll give you what you want, but it will take a few minutes," came out of Sarah's surprised mouth.

"You've got one minute for me to see results." To drive his point home Sergei sliced a 3-inch trench into Sarah's arm.

Phoenix screamed in pain, yet through a combination of will, anger, and a healthy dose of hatred, accomplished exactly the opposite result of Sergei's sadistic intention. She found herself in a Secret Service agent's mind as he sat slumped forlornly on the couch in the Oval Office. Because of the assassination of the President on his watch and the mountain of pent-up anger he felt for missing his chance to save her, the wound up coil of suppressed energy sprang into action at the plea that exploded in his head.

He charged into Sarah's office with his weapon raised. When he saw the bloody letter opener and the stream of blood that flowed from Sarah's arm, he didn't hesitate to pump three bullets rapid-fire into poor Tom's shocked face.

Phoenix felt a wave of adrenaline wash over her, before collapsing to the floor in a heap before Sean Anthony could catch her.

Sean Anthony realized he had made a terrible mistake. True he hadn't any other option when he put Phoenix front and center, but with Aaron now able to reach out to others through Sergei, Aaron now had the means to access psychopathic individuals to attack those of Phoenix's lineage. Subjecting Sergei's brutality on the nerds would be a massacre. He needed to counter, and counter fast or accept he was condemning hundreds of innocents to a brutal death.

Repercussions swept all the way into the 1492 and 1942 realities as 12,000 people dropped dead in a flash, while another 12,000 screamed in horror at the vision of Tom's face exploding.

———◆———

Sean and Alicia stood at the door to Rebecca's room in the Enterprise Sickbay, while Alicia interrogated the poor doctor. "You're telling me you couldn't find anything physically wrong to explain her injuries?"

"Barring a complete autopsy, which I don't think you want me to perform at this time," Dr. Evans sarcastically replied. "I cannot identify why Dr. Cutler had such a violent seizure, and without that knowledge all we can do is wait and see. Dr. Cutler hasn't had any more episodes since we sedated her, so all we can do for now is, continue to monitor her."

Sean softly grabbed Alicia's arm and tried to steer her toward the door. "Thank you, Dr. Evans."

Alicia looked down at Rebecca, who, if she didn't know better, looked like she was in the middle of an afternoon nap. "It isn't fair that such a well put together young lady should have to endure so much crap."

"Everyone to whom much was given, of them much will be required," Sean mused.

This brought a smile to Alicia's face. "Look at you quoting from Luke."

"Reformed Catholic, remember."

Though it was only an hour since Forrest found Rebecca violently shaking on the floor next to her desk, time had slowed to a crawl.

"That pretty well sums up everyone we know in a nutshell. Here we are in the middle of the Mediterranean without the only person capable of communicating with what she claims to be a Carl Eddington possessed Specter." This brought up another thing that bugged Alicia. "If he is here and running interference for us, why did he let anyone attack her?"

"Maybe he knew she would be okay. Maybe Bowie and Franklin are involved. All we know for sure is the path is clear for us to move ahead," Sean offered optimistically. Though he wished he could do more to sympathize, they needed to push ahead. "By the way, Tony is working with Captain Nelson and Commander Thornton to put together the strike force for Rome."

"So what do you think happens when we take over the Vatican?" a worried Alicia asked. "Do we rule this reality for the next nine years like Rebecca did in 1942, or go back home to jail or worse? Honestly Sean, I don't see how this ends well for any of us."

Sean smiled, and gave her a quick kiss. "All I know is Renée came back from the dead. If that can happen, maybe there is a little slice of heaven already laid out and ready for us. One step at a time."

They were about to leave Rebecca when the Sickbay phone rang. Alicia could hear Captain Osaka's voice from three feet away, and he wasn't reporting good news. "When did this happen, and how many are involved?"

This time when he grabbed Alicia's arm, Sean lacked the same gentle touch. "We've got to hurry. Fights have broken out among several crewmembers, and none of it makes any sense. We are taking more casualties."

Sean Anthony held Phoenix tightly in his grasp as the adrenaline rush from her traumatic experience in the White House slowly subsided. "I am so sorry you had to go through that. I should have known Aaron could use the same method as soon as he discovered what we did."

As Phoenix struggled to control the flood of emotions the assault triggered among the many personalities she continued to possess, Sean Anthony tried to find a way forward that would redirect the assault. He needed more time and connections he feared to use, so to spare the child and all the others of her lineage any more grief, he acted to disconnect the shared awareness.

Aaron watched with fascination as Sergei writhed in pain from the impact of the bullets. Sweating profusely the Russian President finally opened his eyes, obviously surprised that he still lived. He leaped out of his chair toward Aaron, who with a mere flick of his wrist stopped him cold. "You have to expect a few bugs, my dear Sergei. Sit down; I'm not through with you yet."

Unfortunately for Sergei, this was only the beginning. Over the next twelve hours, Aaron forced the power hungry leader to reach as far as he could into every connection he could find. When he finished, thousands of the world's most twisted minds had whatever stopped had them from launching into a homicidal rage removed, freeing them to commit horrific acts of violence against whoever happened to be in their path.

Aaron especially enjoyed the crippling effect this had on Sergei each time the authorities managed to violently end their rampages. Satisfied this would continue without any further direction from him. Aaron left Sergei alone to suffer thousands more deaths. "Couldn't happen to a nicer guy."

Aaron put his feet up on the desk in the Oval Office and surveyed the empty room. "This would have been a hell of a lot more fun if we had this battle during the Roman Empire." Visions of thousands of crucifixions that went on for miles as soldiers raped and killed every citizen in a conquered province brought tears of joy to his eyes.

When Sean and Alicia arrived in the CIC, Tony was right in the middle of the action. He signaled for Sean to give him a second while he finished listening to the latest report, this one from the Chancellorsville, before he reported. "Bat-shit crazy is the only way to explain it. Apparently, soon after Dr. Cutler went down, spontaneous fights broke out in every quarter of the fleet.

"The odd thing about it is it sounded like a bad remake of Revenge of the Nerds, with all the geeks picking fights with every Marine and Special Force member they could find. You can imagine how well that turned out for them. Fortunately for all concerned the Marines were too busy laughing to do any real damage, so there were only minor injuries." Tony found it difficult not to laugh at the image of trained fighters eating a sandwich in one hand, while holding his other one on the top of the nerd's head as the geek flailed away ineffectually, Elmer Fudd style.

Sean didn't see the humor. "Do you have an idea about how long until we get the situation under control?"

"You haven't heard the weirdest part yet. All at once, every fight ended, and none of those involved had a clue about what they were doing or why."

The personnel in the CIC must have conjured the same mental picture as Tony because an undercurrent of laughter began to break out. This didn't go over well with Sean. "Important members under my command had their lives put at risk from a source we can't identify. Do you think it will be funny when one of your best friends attacks you? Let's focus people."

Everyone turned their attention back to work, as Alicia looked around the room and decided to offer a rather obvious theory. "When President Harrison used the terror card to launch her coup, remember she sent the military after the geeks first. It is fairly obvious these are the only people who could have threatened her authority."

Tony wasn't convinced. "If that were the case, why didn't the attacks begin as soon as we arrived here?"

"Maybe something changed there. Maybe what Captain Eddington and his son are in the middle of is so damn important they had to stick us here. Think about it. We all lived most of our lives watching our leadership spiral into abject corruption with complete impotence to do anything but talk about it. Seems to me there are some very powerful people, or entities, fully engaged working to change that, and other powerful people, or entities are fighting back. I wish we had a crystal ball to see what was happening back home."

As Alicia continued, she pointed out to Sean. "You reached your ceiling because of your moral compass, and made no bones about it. Then they give you command of an experiment that was meant to fail, and instead we wind up rearranging the entire geopolitical structure in a different reality. We come home to our world and it is imploding like a black hole, and bam, 1492. It's got to be all related to what is happening back home."

The rest of the members of the CIC sat uncomfortably listening to their senior commanders bounce esoteric theory around like escapees from a Malibu rehabilitation center.

"That could explain how some of it is connected, but what does 1942, 2018, and 1492 have to do with each other? On their own, each is significant, but I don't see how changing either 1942 or 1492..." Sean stopped short.

"What is it? What are you thinking?" Tony knew that look on Sean's face.

"Could it be that simple? Think about it. Two pivotal moments in the evolution of humanity brought about because of the destruction of entire societies, with only two numbers inverted in their dates. You all know I believe in a what goes around comes around version of metaphysics, so maybe this will lead to the ultimate destruction of human civilization in 2018. You can only put off a reckoning for so long."

Alicia sat heavily into the nearest chair. "You're saying God is at the bottom of all of this, and we are living in the final days? This isn't exactly how I imagined such an event, but..."

At that moment, the door to the CIC swung open, and barely dressed in a hospital gown stood Rebecca. "Not God, more like us, if we lived millions of years and got bored with all of our toys. Can someone get me a cup of coffee, please?" She plopped down next to a surprised Alicia.

For the first time, Sean thought about how all of this looked to the rest of the CIC crew, and decided it would be best if they continued the conversation in private. "Inform me when Captain Nelson and Commander Thornton are available to join us in the Admirals Ready Room." Sean motioned for Tony to help the still heavily medicated Rebecca follow Alicia, Renée, and him out of the CIC.

As was the custom, when they arrived in the Admirals Quarters, Sean passed out tumblers to everyone. When he saw that Alicia was about to object, Tony countered, "If getting boozed up was good enough for the Constitutional Congress, it is good enough for us."

Sean on the other hand needed to get straight to the point, that is, if Rebecca could maintain coherence. "So what have you neglected to tell us Rebecca? I mean beyond that Commander Eddington is responsible for our being here, and that he is Specter's creator, your husband, and the father of your son we've never met that shares his father's propensity for manipulating time and space?"

Though her Sickbay doctor would be mortified if he knew, Rebecca downed her drink, handed it back to Tony for more, and quickly downed it immediately after he handed back it to her. "Everything you said is the truth, only..." Rebecca stopped and waved her hands up and down signaling her confusion about how much she could say after Carl warned her it was important not to.

Tony handed her a fresh drink, which she quickly downed again, and its effect was immediate as Rebecca melted into the couch. They watched her struggle to fight through the haze, slapping her own face before continuing in a meandering manner. "All I can tell you is that right before I went unconscious, that is, the last time I went unconscious if you know what I mean. It felt like there were thousands of voices in my head, all of them terrified at the sight of a man's head exploding all over them. I mean Gallagher mallet to a water mellow exploding." Her head tilted to the side with a shocked expression on her face. "The even stranger aspect of the experience was that I wasn't here, but back where we belong in 2018. When I woke up they were all gone, like it never happened."

Alicia got up, grabbed a blanket from the bedroom, and threw it over the inebriated scientist. "Pretty much what happened throughout the fleet. Did you recognize any of these people?"

Rebecca seemed to get a second wind. "All I know for sure is that whatever we do here, what they do back home, and what happens in the 1940s reality cannot interfere with each other at the level Carl, Sean Anthony, Bowie, Franklin, and Jesus are playing. Carl only stuck around as long as he could to make sure I was safe, but he had to leave under the same agreement Jesus got that stopped the attacks on us."

"So what did that have to do with me playing god to the Taíno for two years? None of this explains why any entity would go through such a convoluted scheme across three realities?"

"Maybe for the same reason they brought me back," Renée countered. "Who's to say if this is a common occurrence for those who lost their way in life and were worth saving?"

"In a just world, those who risk everything to speak truth to power should be the ones reaping the rewards, yet the opposite is true. Though none of us are saints, we all have a very active conscience, which usually puts us at odds with authority," Alicia answered as she grabbed Sean's arm and led him to sit around the conference table. "Off the top of my head everything we have witnessed so far suggests that we are in the middle of some cosmic pushback."

"Tilled ground. This is what we tried to do in 1942," Sean pointed to Rebecca who sleeping soundly on the couch, "and what sleeping beauty here continued after we left. What was that? A trial run for 1492, and if so, is that what is in store for us, an endless series of screwed up realities?"

"Yeah, all with one thing in common, the constant reminder about the cruelty of humans," Tony responded with sarcasm, as he tipped his tumbler to drain it.

"Yet for lack of any other options, Tony, we persevere. Who knows, maybe when this is all over we will take our place alongside Aristotle, Galileo, and Gloria Steinem." Alicia laughed at the thought the world would glorify any of them, outside of Rebecca.

Alicia's idea brought up something that bothered Renée. "The only thing we know for sure is that according to Franklin, I was brought back as a reward for Tony's efforts. How's that for the ultimate form of sexism. I'm only here because a man wanted me back."

"You go girl." Alicia gave Renée a high five. "I think that was the most sensible thing I have heard from anyone yet, deities, if that is what they are, included."

Tony wasn't happy with the direction this conversation had taken. "You make it sound as if the only reason I wanted you back was to be my girl, when nothing could be further from the truth. More than anything else I missed your friendship and everything you brought to the team."

Renée walked up to Tony and gave him a kiss on his forehead. "The criticism is directed at Franklin and his 18th Century view, not you honey."

Tony smiled and returned the kiss. "Compassion and understanding is what drives all of us, that and getting in as much trouble as legally possible in the attempt." That brought out a smattering of laughter, but also the energy in the room began to calm down.

Always on point, Sean felt it important to remind everyone of the other side. "I think that is a great way to spin it, but none of it makes up for the hundreds of good men and women we lost in the previous attacks."

Rebecca opened her eyes and tried to stand up, but failed and fell back onto the couch. "Not only here Admiral, but also back home, and only my husband and son know what is going on in my home away from home. Imagine if freak city is happening across all the realities that are likely swirling all around us."

Rebecca poked her finger in the air around her as if she could magically stick it into another reality. "So let's go end the slavery the church holds over this time and space and forget about what happens anywhere we can't control." Rebecca once again attempted to get up, but once again fell back onto the couch, this time for good. With her eyes closed and a silly smile on her face, she went silent.

Like a scene change in a TV show, the phone rang. Alicia picked it up, and after listening for a moment reported to Sean. "It's Captain Nelson. He and Commander Thornton are ready to join us."

"Send them ahead." Sean stood up and looked down at Rebecca. "For now, we will take your advice, but so help me, *Doctor*, if we get hammered from out of nowhere again, I will want the rest of what you are holding back from us. Is that clear?"

Without opening her eyes, she nodded yes. Then with her eyes still closed, she tried to get up, but Sean held her back.

"You need to get some rest."

Rebecca struggled against him to rise. "I should go back to see if Specter has picked up anything new." What she really wanted was to see if Carl would return to explain what happened, because the vision of the poor man's head exploding though diluted by the alcohol was still severely freaking her out.

Sean was adamant. "Not going to happen. Renée is going to take you to your cabin and keep you company in case you are still under threat. You two seem to be sharing similar thoughts. Maybe you can come up with some other helpful insights."

Tony was about to object, but Renée cut him off. "Don't worry, if they wanted me dead, I would still be dead."

As Renée helped Rebecca through the door, Commander Thornton and Captain Nelson arrived, both men concerned about Rebecca's wellbeing. Renée gave a quick synopsis of her condition.

"Why don't I help you get her to her cabin?" Captain *Dash* Nelson enjoyed his image as the gallant warrior, and played it up as if he had viewed Top Gun once too often. Right down to the sparkling teeth Renée could not stop looking at.

"That's just not natural," she thought transfixed. "I bet they glow in the dark when he brushes them." Renée tried to shake off his charisma. "No thank you Captain, I've got it."

Thorny shook his head in disgust and pushed Nelson through the door. "Your Commanding Officer demands your presence Ace," Thorny sarcastically exclaimed, as the door closed behind them.

"Men can be such assholes," Rebecca said without raising her head.

"Amen to that, sister." Renée wrapped her arm around Rebecca's waist for support as they stumbled their way down the corridor.

"We have a serious problem, people. We have to go back to the cave in China so you can get your overfed asses back to work."

"Only if you can get us to where I can gain access to an internet hub," Phoenix interjected.

Sean Anthony decided it was time to see what his acolyte could come up with, and lead from behind. "What do you have in mind?"

"I installed a backdoor into my virus. However, we will have to break in to the NSA server room to access it."

"That's my girl," Sean Anthony thought. "As soon as we make the move to do so, Aaron will know, so we won't have much time."

Phoenix gave him a look as if to say, *are you kidding me?* She then pulled a USB flash drive from her pocket. "I won't need but a few minutes. Just insert, tap a few commands and we are gone. Once we regain control of our uplinks from the cave to the NSA servers we can do almost anything you want."

As soon as everyone had gathered their belongings, the green mist swirled. A split second later, Sean Anthony and Phoenix were in the NSA server room where the virus had launched. Phoenix plugged the flash drive into the nearest computer, and when satisfied with the transfer, she typed in two IP addresses. "All finished. I added a little something extra that will be impossible for anyone but me to find."

Sean Anthony was about to transport them out when the door to the room they were in opened and Aaron walked in.

Sean Anthony decided to have a little fun, and quickly modified his plans. "Off you go," and in a flash Phoenix disappeared. Slowly the room they stood in faded away, leaving the two antagonists floating in one of the chambers of the International Space Station, much to the shock of those occupying it. Sean Anthony magnified their shock when he snapped his fingers and they found themselves back home.

Aaron floated his way to one of the portals, and peered out at the blue planet. "You know we are going to have stop meeting like this, though I have enjoyed the solitude of space from time to time."

Sean Anthony directed his view out into space. "It's too bad we always find ourselves on the opposite sides of creation, and always with the drama. Just once I wish you wouldn't feel like every atom of reality has to bend to your will."

Aaron scoffed. "You are the one that decided to break the rules. If the others knew, you know they would call an end to the whole experience, and your precious planet and all the realities here would cease to exist. All I have to do is give a quick shout-out and poof."

Sean Anthony laughed off the threat. "It's not like you have forgotten the time you took out an entire sector of time and space, which by the way included you know who's favorite creations, and I kept quiet. Besides, you know as well as I do the others already know. They just don't care enough to intercede."

It was Aaron's turn to laugh. "Then why was your dad concerned enough to bring you in through your mortal mother, who by the way is creating her own set of problems in that other made up reality you put her in. What's up with that? Do you think by creating new realities will affect the outcome in any way?"

They both passed through the chamber's wall into space where Sean Anthony floated up to Aaron. "What I *will* create in this particular end is a place where maybe we can learn something new, because frankly brother, we all need to move on."

"Though I will admit the last million years or so haven't been especially progressive, there isn't any way the others will risk what you and your father are attempting. With the knowledge of what happened the last time someone was foolish enough to try, they don't want to challenge the existing order and risk what they control."

Aaron snapped his fingers, and the shockwave of a star in a full-blown supernova explosion buffeted them. "What do you think the last thoughts of the billions of lifeforms were when this baby blew them into oblivion? I'll tell you what they should have contemplated. That time and space didn't leave even the slightest trace of their existence once their worlds were incinerated?"

Sean Anthony felt the atoms from the exploding star pass through him, and as they did, he pieced together fragments of memories, which he molded into a physical form that now floated between them. The lifeform was remarkable in that it would have fit in well among the Earth's land-dwelling denizens. Face, torso, bipedal, though the combinations of scales with feathers gave it a unique beauty.

Before it could acknowledge its newfound resurrection, Aaron dispersed its atoms back into the cloud. "Just like you to want to save stray puppies. Unlike you, and like most of our peers, I prefer to keep those who went extinct and all of their memories to keep expanding outward with the rest of the universe. Reruns always bored me."

"Yet here we are," Sean Anthony countered, "a perfect example of our own hypocrisy. We were given the time to evolve, but we deem no one else worthy of the same."

This elicited another round of laughter from Aaron." Like an exploding star is what kills off your current pets? Even without my exquisite intervention, they were doing a fine enough job of ending their existence before ever getting close to the end of their star's three billion remaining years of life. At least the creature you reassembled wasn't trying to kill off everything in sight."

Sean Anthony shook his head no. "Stuck in instinct, the creature also lacked the passion and curiosity that would have allowed it to evolve past its current form. The potential for other species to evolve to our level or beyond is the part that threatens both your and the other's sense of superiority in our little corner of space and time. God forbid our kind should ever strive for more."

Aaron snapped his fingers and the view expanded to show the Milky Way from a distance in deep space. "You call this the road to nowhere. Look around you. With a mere thought we can go anywhere in the galaxy, all because we had the genius to figure out how to interact with every one of the elements in it.

"You want something that was decided millions of years ago to change, which unfortunately for your pets simply isn't meant to be. Durius built them for our entertainment, which if I am not mistaken was the only way the others would give permission to splice some of our genes into them in the first place. By the way, don't you find it narcissistic of you that you wish more for them?"

"Or maybe they have helped connect me back to a part of my soul that used to question our place in the big picture," Sean Anthony reminisced. "Before you laugh at the idea, when was the last time anyone but dad tried to discover some other way to use our vast knowledge other than merely showing off?"

"Just because we enjoy the view from our corner of the Milky Way, does not mean we need to go around interacting with the billions of others across space to prove ourselves."

As Aaron spoke, Sean Anthony returned them to the moment of the Big Bang. "You're not the least bit curious about what lies beyond?"

This brought sarcastic laughter from Aaron. "We have billions of years before all the lights go off, so what's the hurry? Besides, you are familiar with the stories about why any further expansion of our collective awareness could end all of existence, including us."

Sean Anthony smiled. "And therein lies the difference between the established order and those like dad and me who wish to stir the pot. For all the grandeur, this universe is still a prison. So what if we know when the universe will end, if we spend all of that time without any passion. As confused and violent as humanity is, I think you would be one of their fiercest defenders, but you are not. You hate them because they can do something we can't; they desire to evolve."

Aaron's turn to smile. "For once you have figured me out. I hate them for their inability to retain even a crumb of an idea that works and stick with it. You call it evolution; I call it attention deficit disorder."

Sean Anthony sighed. "This universe has consumed half of its energy and reached middle age. Our end will not be any different just because we measure our lifespan in billions of years and theirs in a millisecond. Who will remember us?"

"Round and round we go, where we stop, I sure as hell don't know." Aaron snapped his fingers one last time. They now stood in the middle of a very nasty landfill in the middle of India. Scores of shabbily clothed men, women, and children rummaged through the rotting remains of trash. "You wish to risk all for a species that does this to one another?"

"In its current state of evolution? Of course not. Selfish, self-centered, self-aggrandizing, racist, sexist, greedy – and that's only the soccer moms. But then again I blame this on you and your kind mucking things up."

Sean Anthony snapped his fingers, and they now stood on a hill overlooking a small primitive village where Imprinter 4, Wisdom, imprinted an ancient female. "You are afraid that little bit of ourselves we gave to humans will evolve in time to threaten your superiority, and more disturbing, the illusion of us as gods will end."

Aaron was unaffected. "And therein lies the rub. I know my place, and that place is with one boot on their neck, and a knife to the throat while I rape their wives and daughters. You on the other hand only wish to take the fun out of it all by building artificial constructs of morality that is contrary to the true nature of the beasts. You are so blinded by your faulty beliefs that you can't see that I merely needed to remove one important political figure to set the whole world on fire. Human nature did the rest."

Sean Anthony didn't bother to argue. "A little revolution, now and then, is a good thing."

Sean Anthony's reaction confused Aaron. "So now you refer to the end of your pets as a little revolution? Well enjoy the final act while you can, because within the next three days it will become much more than little." With a flash, Aaron disappeared.

Sean Anthony smiled as if satisfied with the results. "Well that should properly motivate him."

Since the Enterprise Task Force had entered the Mediterranean, the shipping traffic had decreased dramatically as local sailors spread the word of the colossal metal monsters. Admiral Sean Phillips, reminded once again of the absurdity of their current situation, had ordered Seahawks to fly ahead to scare all shipping out of the way of their faster moving ships. The bizarre flying dragons with earth-rattling noise emanating from their rapidly spinning blades scattered the 15th Century sailors at speeds best described as humorlessly slow.

Within the first 24 hours of their entrance into the Mediterranean, the 15th Century sailors, the most superstitious of the day, shared their stories, each one adding their own embellishments to the narrative. It didn't take long for the nearby port dwellers to run for the hills with nightmares of giant beasts swooping down from the sky to roast them alive and eat them.

Fortunately, news in the 15th Century traveled at the speed of horseback, so Italy remained uninformed of their existence. Having cleared the Strait of Bonifacio between Corsica and Sardinia, they were now within one hundred fifty miles of their objective, Vatican City. In the Enterprise CIC, Tony briefed Sean and Alicia on the plan to take the Vatican and capture the Pope.

"Commander Thornton will lead a team of 30 SEALs deployed on 6 MH-60 Seahawk helicopters from the Enterprise and Chancellorsville, and land in Saint Peter's Square at 0200 hours for the ultimate element of surprise. We figure they should have complete control of the entire compound by 0300."

"How many casualties do you expect?" Alicia was worried about the attack turning into a bloodbath.

Tony hesitated, unsure how she was going to react to answer.

"That bad?" Alicia's worried look deepened.

"Initially, yes. However, to make sure the fighting ends quickly, Commander Thornton and I agreed we have to hit them hard and fast, so we take the fight out of the rest of the defenders. As primitive as 15th Century weaponry is, a well-placed musket shot will still kill. We hope that once we get inside, stun guns will suffice from there."

"Thank you, Tony. With a squadron of F-35s overhead at dawn, the rest of the population should be properly impressed enough to keep their heads down." Sean got up from the desk to stretch. "That will be all for now. Everyone get some sleep."

Sean and Tony watched the warriors file into the Seahawks from Vultures Row, a balcony platform with a great view of the flight deck. Now fifty miles off the coast and an hour before the attack, the noise from the three Seahawk's spinning rotors had everyone's adrenaline pumping.

"Almost makes me wish I was with them," Tony reminisced.

Without turning to face him, Sean retorted, "That it is killing you that I won't let you, is more like it."

The last of the SEALs turned and waved a thumbs-up to them before disappearing into the craft.

"Bring them all home safely, Thorny," Sean said softly.

Tony shared Sean's sentiment. "Amen to that."

Moments later, one by one the Seahawks lifted off the deck and disappeared into the darkness.

Half an hour later the attack group went *feet dry* 1,000 feet above the rural landscape below. Fifteen minutes later, the outlines of the city began to appear on the horizon, their target now only minutes away. Gear checks commenced among those who would be storming the bastion of this era's political hierarchy. Conversation remained light, as each member tried to digest the magnitude of what they were about to attempt. "Target in sight," came over the intercoms.

On the lead chopper, Thorny reminded his men, "First ones in, first ones out."

They could see Saint Peter's Square below rapidly getting larger as they approached. Then the chopper rapidly dropped in elevation until it abruptly hit the ground only moments later. "Move, move, move!" Thorny yelled as he literally pushed his squad off the Seahawk.

The guards that stood at the main entryways into the sprawling complex only had time to wipe their tired eyes in disbelief at the sight of the monsters landing in front of them before the SEALs were on them. Contrary to Tony's grim predictions, none had a chance to think about challenging the heavily armed SEALs covered in their body armor, which the defenders could only imagine was the skin of alien monsters.

In the Enterprise CIC, Sean, Alicia, and Tony watched real-time video via links set up through an orbiting E2D Advanced Hawkeye, as the thirty SEALs spread throughout the complex to secure their objectives.

In the first five minutes, many guards hit the ground in convulsions as Commander Thornton's SEAL squad tasked with capturing the Pope hit them with the electric darts from their stun guns. Ahead of schedule, they entered the Papal Apartments. After a quick search of the adjoining rooms, they came upon a set of heavy double doors. When opened, the sight in front of everyone's eyes was as comedic as anything Saturday Night Live could have lampooned. Pope Alexander VI, the most corrupt pontiff in history, woke up in shock surrounded by three women, ranging from 12 to 20 years old, not a stitch of clothing among them.

"Good evening, Your Eminence. Is this a bad time?" Under most conditions, Commander Thornton's countenance would exude restraint, yet it took all of his energy to control the laughter that welled up at the sight of the saggy, wrinkled old man in front of him.

The mere fact anyone would invade his inner sanctum was

enough for the shocked Pope Alexander to let loose with a stream of Italian invectives, some of which Thorny actually understood. This, when added to the screams of the three naked girls who jumped out of the bed and clumsily fumbled for clothing to cover their bodies, was enough for Thorny to hit the Pope with his stun gun rather than wait for the interpreter. Oddly enough watching the Pope jerk around in agony slowed the girls down as they smiled at their abuser's discomfort. The late arriving interpreter reassured them that they were not about to suffer the same fate, so they thankfully finished dressing and rushed out of the room.

Thorny keyed his mic. "Sacred Cow is in custody, and for now unconscious and naked."

Upon receiving Thorny's oddly worded confirmation, Sean turned to Alicia. "We don't want to know, do we?"

Alicia shook her head. "No, we don't. It's time to go."

After they left the CIC, Sean gave her a thorough look over. "It's been quite some time since I've seen you in combat fatigues. I approve of the look, but are you sure this is the first impression you want to make? I mean if you wanted to get their attention, a queen wrapped in velvet and silk with a crown to match would suit the era better."

Tony followed with his own inspection. "I don't know Sean, looks to me like she nailed it. She gets to rub the nose in it of every chauvinistic pig who has beaten, raped, or made women work as chattel under the authority of God, while showing a total disregard for being sexually desirable."

Alicia punched Tony on the shoulder. "You only wish you could look half as good as I do." Alicia stopped and stroked her sides up to her breasts to accent the obvious. "But seriously the both of you better keep us well supplied because we are not touching any food, wine, or water from any other source. These people are the ones who perfected the art of sudden unexplained deaths among the ruling elite."

"We are leaving the Cesar Chavez, Patuxent, and Decatur to keep the helos fueled, and you and the rest of the ground force well fed and armed until we return," Tony reminded her. "However, if there is trouble the Decatur can't handle, the cavalry is just over the horizon."

They continued to the flight deck, where Alicia didn't waste any time boarding. With a thumbs-up from Sean, the pilot lifted off the deck. "God, I can't wait to see the video of her encounter with Pope Alexander for the look on his face."

As they approached the Vatican in the early morning haze, Alicia peered out the helicopter's window to see about a thousand of the local inhabitants neither protesting nor celebrating; they were all praying. The pilot set the bird down near the entrance to Saint Peter's Basilica, and immediately took off for the return trip after Alicia and her belongings disembarked.

Commander Thornton stood twenty feet away as sailors grabbed her baggage. Alicia walked over and returned the salute he gave her. "Unconscious and naked?"

"You had to be there. I have the footage if you want a good laugh."

"I think it would be better if I meet him first. It's going to be hard enough to take him seriously without what I can only imagine are horrific images," Alicia replied with a frown, as she motioned for him to lead the way.

When they entered the room Thorny had placed him in earlier, the look on his face was even better than advertised. Alicia didn't waste any time displaying her sexuality and her superiority over the diminutive despot. "What's the matter, Your Unholiest? Not your type?" Though Alicia spoke fluent Italian, the dialect had evolved some since the 15th Century. That and the after effects of the Taser left the Pope with little to say. "I doubt you were so quiet when you handed down numerous extremely painful death sentences during your reign merely for your perverse pleasure."

Alicia walked around the simple folding metal chair he sat on. To rob Pope Alexander further of his sense of power, Alicia had him striped and dressed in an orange one-piece prison jumpsuit.

"Are you worried we plan to reciprocate in kind?" She grabbed the back of the chair, and spun it around to face her. "If you are not, you should be, because we have big plans for you."

Alicia took a moment to take in the grandeur of the room. "Just think, instead of boiling you in hot oil in the middle of the square, which by the way was what *I* wanted to do, instead we are going to keep you right here. For reasons I am still trying to fathom, my husband thinks you would much rather cooperate than have us turn you over to those your rule has crippled the most. So what do you think, a slow tortuous death or go out on the balcony to explain to your flock, and the Kings and Queens of Europe, the dramatic vision from God you have received?"

This got the man's attention, and for being a high-functioning sociopath, he was noticeably relaxed. "What are your terms?"

An hour later, the documents signed by the Pope, and in the custody of the Pontiff's terrified personal emissary, were airborne and headed to the Enterprise. Alicia then spent the afternoon with the Pope going over the speech he was to give the next morning. Earlier that morning, she sent the cowering lower level church officials into the populace to announce the upcoming event.

During the day and into the evening, Seahawk helicopters ferried to the Vatican the Marines, and Navy support staff, plus equipment and supplies the Admiral's Staff figured would suffice as an occupying force. The SEALs and Commander Thornton returned to the Enterprise as the Marines replaced them.

When Sean Anthony returned to the cave in China, he found Phoenix and Adonis huddled together talking in a rapid-fire exchange that could only mean one thing. "It worked?" he asked.

"Better than I hoped," Phoenix answered. "Not only can we control most of their computer equipped communications and armaments networks, I got us into the Joint Chief of Staff's internal networks, and you will not believe what they have done."

Sean Anthony couldn't resist. "They took over the government, and now all pretense of civilian authority is over."

Phoenix looked like someone had smashed her computer with a hammer. "Party pooper. However, I bet you didn't know they had all the members of Congress are locked up at the Greenbrier. Yes, that Greenbrier we were in only a few days ago. Ironic isn't it that they would be imprisoned in a place that was originally built to save their asses."

Adonis leaned back in his chair with his fingers locked behind his head. "Look, I got the part where we became a part of Phoenix, and the bit with the President's bitch, but what I don't get is who is the cat that showed up at the NSA and made you do your magic thing to send little missy to the cave without you?"

Adonis' street smarts had deduced this was Aaron. "He's the one, isn't he? And he can pull off all the same crazy shit you do."

"His name is Aaron, and yes he is the one who has spent most of his miserable life dreaming up new and innovative ways to destroy all of you."

Sean Anthony figured this was a good time to bring his team up to date with another piece of the story. "Aaron and others who are like-minded don't believe any of you should have ever existed, so needless to say, with all the powers at their disposal, their actions have created serious consequences for humanity. As you have probably figured out by now, we are rapidly arriving at the conclusion of this long, hard-fought battle. Though I have placed much responsibility on all of you, if we don't, and I mean mostly all of you, come up with a counter that will bring the violence to an end, this planet will find new tenants and mankind will be erased."

"So in other words, asteroids had nothing to do with the dinosaurs going belly up?"

"Precisely, Mr. Adonis." However, Sean Anthony could not resist adding, "However, isn't it rather presumptuous of you to assume they no longer exist?"

Rather than wait for Adonis to finish chewing on that little nugget, Sean Anthony continued to challenge the group. "So what do you have for me?" Though Sean Anthony had a fallback plan, he figured now wound be a good time to see if the most intelligent youth of their generation could give Aaron a run for his over-bloated ego on their own.

Throughout the ensuing conversation, Phoenix remained fixed on typing out code to integrate their backdoor connection to the NSA servers. With a final flourish, she triumphantly announced to the group, "We now have access to all the major media networks, including their satellite uplinks, and we can do something the Pentagon can't. We can communicate with their subordinates. So who do we send the Predator drones after first, Wall Street, or the Koch Brothers?"

Sean Anthony had a better idea. "So now you have everything you could ever dream of. Your entire argument as Black Hats was to facilitate the overthrow of the corrupt overlords to return power to the people." He paused as he walked around the different hackers at their workstations, making sure he had their complete attention.

"That mission has been accomplished. Now what?"

Any sense of elation over Phoenix's news immediately ended, replaced with the immense responsibility that now lay squarely on their young shoulders.

Sean Anthony enjoyed their muted response for a moment with the full knowledge that they were feeling for the first time how truly monumental their undertaking was. When satisfied that this reality was firmly set in their minds, he gave them a nudge in the right direction. "Considering we can now control the message, what do you suggest that message be? However, keep in mind the successful message of conformity every empire has used over the last four thousand years to control the masses did nothing but ensure the power of those in charge of the empire. Another cult of personality or a misleading statement of equality of the masses, is that what you want to repeat? Is it going to be the same world order, same old structured propaganda, and most importantly, the same old male emperors giving the same old orders?"

All eyes followed Sean Anthony as he walked around the room. "Or do you find a way to accomplish the impossible, and that is to turn an entire society against centuries of indoctrination?"

Phoenix jumped on the idea. "The only way to begin to do that would be for the world to see the United States of America actually behaving as the one its apologists have so successfully sold to its citizens."

Adonis quickly saw a problem with this logic. "That would be a great idea if you didn't first have to spend a month explaining to the public all the despicable things done in their names over the last seventy-five years. Let's face it; there isn't any way to excuse the criminality once you open that door."

Then from the farthest corner, a young Vietnamese programmer who rarely spoke up added her concern. "Besides, with the population already cynical because of their years of acceptance of such a sorry state of affairs, why would they believe we are any different?"

This led to every one of the geeks adding to the list of problems that Phoenix's idea would create. Sean Anthony smiled as the list continued to expand over the next twenty minutes. He decided to let it play out, taking a moment to enjoy the passion that was on full display.

As she looked around the room, satisfied that everyone was truly engaged in resolving the problem, Phoenix calmly returned to her work. The sight of the pale little slip of a white girl giving everyone a lesson in perspective, immediately refocused the group, who all followed suit to try to find an answer to the dilemma.

Phoenix glanced over at Sean Anthony, who smiled and gave her a wink of approval.

Over the next six hours, Phoenix and Adonis energetically divvied up different tasks among the group, which then split into smaller groups as they pooled information back and forth.

All the while, Sean Anthony stood admiring how well this perfect mix of personalities and talent worked with each other. This time he wouldn't become directly involved, which would help to keep Aaron from directly challenging their success.

Over the next eighteen hours, Sean Anthony stood by while the group feverishly worked to find as many ways as they could to maximize their use of the White House and NSA files they had downloaded while Phoenix controlled the President's Secretary. The realization that this generation communicated across their shared network at the speed of light compared to the snail's pace of their parent's era of technology fascinated him. Except for the occasional *Sheit* and *Fuckin A*, the only other sounds were computer fans keeping rhythm with the thousands of keystrokes.

When the group stopped to compare notes, the true scope of the Executive Branch betrayal came to view. Phoenix and Adonis then focused their efforts on the audio of the President's conversations with her Chief of Staff, Aaron, and this is when Phoenix found her eureka moment. She removed her ear buds, and turned the audio up. "You guys have got to hear this. You want to know who gave the orders to set off the nuke in San Francisco?"

That was their last spoken words for the next six hours, until finally after two cases of Cheetos, twenty boxes of Cinnamon Pop Tarts, and enough Red Bull to send a herd of elephants on a rampage, Adonis looked over to Phoenix, and asked her, "Do you want to do the honors?"

"Age before beauty, Mr. Mean and Nasty."

Adonis smiled at the dig, as he informed the group, "So, not only can we remotely reboot the internet grid, we can simultaneously piggyback our malware that will allow only us to dictate who can receive and send data and communications. Badda bing, badda boom, game over."

"Time to rock n roll?" Phoenix addressed the question to Sean Anthony.

"It's your show. Let the fun begin."

She hit Enter on her keyboard and the new virus began to work its way through the backdoor she had installed on the NSA servers where every connected portal came alive and quickly uploaded it. Within thirty minutes, everything in the world with a computer chip had a new master.

In his cabin on board the Seawolf, Captain Mark Daily needed a drink, though with a few exceptions, the US Navy had banned alcohol on ships since 1914. As Commander of the northern element, he would be the one giving orders to the English nobility, and he had absolutely no idea who was who, and more importantly who was trying to do what to each other. The stack of historical documents Alicia and Renée had put together before the task force left Cuba proved to be more of a headache than help, what with all of their internecine conflicts.

Commander Wesley Brenner watched his Captain stare at the offending papers. "To tell you the truth, I don't know why you are so concerned. Who cares about the Tudors, Yorks, or who the legitimate ruler is? Once we show up off the mouth of the River Thames it will all be irrelevant anyway."

"You of all people should know how ridiculous you sound; of course it matters. It matters that Richard III murdered the twin Princes in the Tower of London to keep the throne. It matters that they were the adored brothers of Queen Elizabeth who will be with King Henry VII when we meet. It matters that Henry is not as despicable as his predecessors, Richard III or IV, and that out of all of this mess the only one I want to deal with is Elizabeth. She at least put others before herself."

"I don't know Skipper. Seems to me you are the lucky one. You only have to deal with the Dutch and British royals, while the Admiral has the rest of Europe, and based on what I read, more pretenders to their crowns than super yachts vying for attention at the Monaco Yacht Show."

Daily looked at his *born silver spoon in mouth* First Officer and wondered how someone so limited in curiosity could rise so high up the ranks. Though competent in the many aspects of his nautical duties, Captain Daily shuddered at the thought of Commander Brenner in command of his boat, which with him stuck presenting their demands to the royals made this necessary. The sound of the intercom interrupted his thoughts.

"You wanted to be notified when we reached the English Channel, Captain. We are ten miles out. Also the Shiloh reports numerous surface contacts that sonar has verified."

"I'll be right there." Then to Brenner he added, "To put it into context for you, Commander, imagine if you had second cousins who lusted after your inheritance and all they had to do to claim it was to convince your wife's mother that if you died she would make sure they got it all, minus her cut. Then all she would have to do is convince her widowed daughter to marry that cousin. These are the waters we are about to sail into."

"She would never…"

"Even with that pre-nup you have in place?"

Brenner said nothing in response. However, now he would spend the next month thinking about what his young bride back home in the 2018 reality was doing with his fortune while he was stuck here in 1492.

Bat Shit Crazy

Their entrance to the English Channel began between the Cornwall Peninsula of England and the Breton Peninsula of France. Within 30 minutes, they encountered the first of the shipping lanes.

"Captain on deck."

"At ease. What's the range to the nearest target?"

"Fifty-five hundred yards and closing, Sir."

"Prepare to surface the boat."

Activity in the control room accelerated as the sailors went about their checklists.

"Surface the boat."

Upon his command, the Seawolf surged upward, and moments later broke the ocean surface. Captain Daily had climbed half the way up the ladder to the conning tower when the Seawolf leveled out. "You're with me Commander."

Within two minutes, multiple binoculars scanned the ocean around them to find the rest of the task force, which included the cruisers Princeton and Shiloh, trailed by the supply ships Laramie and Norman Schwarzkopf 500 yards astern. "Have the Shiloh lead the task force single file and follow our course. Increase speed to 20 knots. Let's make ourselves known."

The reaction of the contacts, which were 15th Century caravel merchant ships and their escort, mirrored those who first caught sight of the Enterprise, a rapid change in course that did nothing to increase their distance from the approaching Seawolf. "Bring us to within 200 yards," Captain Daily relayed down. "Might as well let them see us as humans."

To his surprise, the activity aboard the single warship escorting the merchants led to them running out her guns, and Daily could see additional sailors lining the rail armed with muskets. The last thing he thought they would do is attack. "So be it," he thought.

Factoring their rapidly closing speed on the sailing ships, Daily needed to decide quickly what his response would be. He couldn't risk a lucky shot disabling his boat, so he turned to his XO and ordered, "Target that warship with a Harpoon and fire when ready."

With some hesitation, Commander Brenner relayed the order before he asked his Captain, "No offense, Sir, but isn't that like swatting a fly with a wrecking ball?"

Captain Daily didn't respond. He focused his binoculars on the 15th Century warship, and could make out clearly the terrified faces of its doomed sailors. He continued to watch as the shudder beneath him signaled the launch of the missile through one of the forward torpedo tubes. A second later, the missile broke through to the surface, blowing its protective cover off as the rocket fired lifting it high in the air. The eyes of the sailors on the French warship went wide as their bodies froze in terror as they followed the missile's rapid rise. It quickly reached the apex of its flight before nosing almost straight down to slam into the wooden ship, sending millions of pieces of the sailors shattered bodies mixed with fragments of their ship soaring into the air. When the smoke cleared, all that remained to identify they were ever there was scattered wreckage.

Captain Daily looked over at his second in command. "We are not here to play patty cake. Anything that threatens either this ship or any under my command will suffer the consequences. I expect nothing less from you. Are we clear mister?"

"Yes Sir."

Daily gave his First Officer a hard look to drive home the point that the safety of his boat came before any thought of mercy toward those they were out to conquer.

"Understood Sir."

Meanwhile, aboard the surviving merchant ships white flags quickly replaced their ship's colors. Without a break in speed to acknowledge the surrendered ships, Daily and his task force continued on course into the channel, much to the relief of those terrified souls. The merchant ships ever so slowly sailed away in all directions of the compass to warn the region of the destructive monsters now within their midst.

That evening, Captain Daily transferred to the Shiloh to finalize how the operation would unfold. Arguments for and against whether to set up a stronghold near the water's edge, or launch a strike while still out in the English Channel, went on through the night.

"I for one would not want to get anywhere near land and take the chance of getting one of the many diseases London was known for during this period. Add in the disgusting reality that they throw their business out of their windows onto the street below, and I think setting up somewhere in the country would be our healthiest option."

Captain Daily turned his gaze from the window to the unrolled map from the era, another of Alicia's gifts, and began to ponder the options he had decided were the most practical. It only took him a moment to reach a decision on which he would order into action. "Not knowing where the King is and according to Alicia's notes, him being of a nasty disposition, we need an emissary to convince the King to parley, and she thinks the perfect candidate would be the Archbishop of Canterbury, Cardinal John Morton."

He then directed his attention to the CIC Officer. "Inform the SEAL Commander that he is the target." Captain Daily pointed to a location on the map. "He can be found here at Lambeth Palace and let's get a Seahawk from the Princeton in the air. I want high altitude reconnaissance over Lambeth Palace and Windsor Castle; I don't want to spook the populace yet."

After the CIC analyzed the reconnaissance information, two more Seahawks lifted off from their respective cruisers, formed up, and headed inland. The countryside below revealed a scene of scattered thatch roofed homes of peasants surrounded by the fields they worked, with not a single sign of technology anywhere to be seen. Twenty minutes later, Lambeth Palace appeared in the window straight ahead; seconds later the two Seahawks hit the ground. Ten SEALs spilled out and headed to their objective, while the Seahawks lifted back up to offer cover.

The few peasants they came across on their way to the brick gatehouse immediately dropped to their knees with their hands covering their faces. When they peeked out to see the monsters run right past them, they ran away as fast as their adrenaline-flooded bodies could carry them.

Unfortunately, this isn't how the Archbishop's guard reacted as a flight of arrows suddenly made their appearance from over the outer wall of the Palace. Before the SEALs on the ground could react, Captain Randy Stone in the lead Seahawk flew over the wall at 200 feet and his gunner let loose deadly fire from its MK-25 6-Barrel Gatling Gun. That was the last of the counter attack.

When the SEALs breached the gateway and entered the courtyard, they witnessed ten bullet-riddled bodies scattered across the ground. Prepared for further attacks, the SEALs cautiously entered the Great Hall, where they were surprised to find a lone man dressed in his church vestments waiting there. "So are you here for my soul?"

This is not what the SEAL squad leader had expected. "No father. We are here to help you and your subjects."

He then keyed his mic. "Shiloh CIC, package secure."

"Roger that."

Seated in the Shiloh CIC, Captain Mark Daily and Captain Henry Jackson had been listening to the reports from the overhead speakers. Daily breathed a sigh of relief. "Now let's see if you can persuade the King's buddy to convince him to parley. If we can't go to Mohammed, maybe we can get Mohammed to come to us. Oh, and you better get ready, because you will handle the negotiations after they bring the Archbishop aboard."

Captain Jackson laughed. "You could have told me that bit of news sooner."

"Who did you think it was going to be – me? No, this negotiation has to between emissaries, you for me, and the Cardinal for the King."

Captain Jackson rose from his seat to leave. "You will be sitting down for dinner at Winsor tonight or my name isn't Kissinger."

"Kissinger? Really?"

"Foster Dulles?"

Daily merely shook his head as Jackson left the CIC, and then addressed the CIC Officer. "Reconnaissance report."

"Review of the reconnaissance video footage revealed only a small force of twenty of the King's Guards plus staff at Winsor Castle, Sir."

Thirty minutes later in the Captains Cabin, Captain Jackson sat across from the shaken but still pious Archbishop. He handed him a glass of the clergyman's wine the SEAL Commander had thoughtfully brought back with them, which the Cardinal willingly took. "First off, let me assure you that it is not our intention to depose either you or the Royal Family. As you might have figured out by now, we are not from around these parts, but let me reassure you that our only reason for being here is to improve the lives of your subjects. Either we can accomplish this through negotiation or by force or arms, and let me assure you that as you have witnessed, we possess weapons that can wipe out the King's army in minutes."

Archbishop Moreton took a moment to ponder Jackson's message and to take measure of the man. "You speak in an interesting English dialect I am not familiar with. Though it may be true what you say, what makes you think I have any sway over His Majesty?"

"Well, you both hated Richard II and IV, not to mention Richard III for sticking you in jail for treason, and now here you are, the most powerful representative of the church under Henry's reign. Besides, I know you are one of the court's closest advisors, and being so, wouldn't it be a good idea to find out as much you can about a force you can't possibly defend against?"

It was Jackson's turn to sit back and take measure of the Cardinal. He could see by the subtle shift of expression on the holy man's face the negotiations were over and it was now a matter of resolving the details.

"To review, we have chosen Windsor Castle as the location for presenting my King Mark to your King Henry. We will take you back to Lambeth so you can send messengers to King Henry, and then you will travel to Windsor.

"Agreed," Archbishop Morton announced. "Now please take me home so I can eat my midday meal."

It took the rest of the day for the Archbishop's messenger to reach the King. It wasn't until early the next morning that reconnaissance overflights confirmed a large body of troops and carriages making their way to Windsor Castle where preparations were ongoing for an audience.

That evening, Captain Mark Daily's Seahawk hovered 200 feet above Windsor, as its blinding searchlight swept in an arc around the castle grounds to magnify their arrival. Aware the King had positioned his army at the three chokepoints leading to the castle, Daily had arranged his own surprise. "Captain Stone, take her down. It's time to rewrite history."

The helicopter slowly lowered to the ground a mere thirty feet from the main door, making sure the side Daily would exit from faced it. When the door opened, *King Mark* jumped out in his finest dress whites, and briskly headed toward the six guards in armor waiting.

He couldn't resist. "Take me to your leader."

Bat Shit Crazy

Once inside, the coldness of the castle's stone construction was his first impression, the second was how many men in armor lined his route. As he exited the grand entry, he found himself in a large room with vaulted ceilings, and at the end stood two elevated thrones, occupied by Henry VII and his beautiful Queen Elizabeth. On both sides and filling out the room stood more knights, nobles, counselors, sycophants, and the London's most powerful merchants.

Daily stopped ten feet short of the steps and smiled. "Thank you, Your Highness, for agreeing to this meeting."

The muffled voices throughout the crowd registered their shock that their mysterious guest failed to bow in the Royal's presence. While Henry looked Daily over in a manner that looked for weakness, Elizabeth's eyes drew the Captain's as she maintained her focus on his. Seeing this, and obviously unhappy about it, Henry finally spoke.

"Though you fly in the sky in machines of metal, and possess weapons beyond my comprehension, I see that you are still only human. So one must ask oneself why would you threaten my people, and then show yourself in front of me alone and apparently unarmed?"

Daily calmly smiled at the King, then reached into his pocket and pulled out his radio. Everyone in the room drew back at the sight of the strange little box, everyone that is except the Queen who appeared more fascinated than afraid. Daily keyed the mic.

"Captain Stone, are you ready?"

"On your order, Sir."

Daily looked up and many were looking around the hall to see where the other voice was coming from. "Give them a show."

Seconds later the sound of gunfire could be heard coming from all four corners of the compass. It continued for exactly thirty seconds, and then stopped as suddenly as it began. "In case you are wondering, that was the sound of only a few of my airships exposing the trap you laid out for me."

Daily watched as Henry clenched hard on the arms of his throne. He ignored that, and contacted Stone. "Status report."

"All three approaches are now clear of troops, Captain, and the King's forces are moving away in a somewhat confused state, over."

Daily then returned his attention back to Henry, and in a mocking voice stated, "You are going to have to learn how to play nice, *Your Highness*." As he finished speaking, they heard a commotion from outside of the hall. Before any of the knights could react, ten armed to the teeth SEALs marched in and took up positions.

Two of the Knights closest drew their swords and charged at the intruders. However, that turned out to be a really-bad idea because of all the metal that encased them. Two SEALs hit the trigger on their stun guns and the darts stuck in the chain mail. After they stopped convulsing and silently lay on the hard floor, you could hear a pin drop in the meeting hall.

"Impressive display of savagery. What is your name, or does your kind name themselves?"

Daily looked up surprised that the comments came from Elizabeth. "Excuse me for my rudeness Your Highness. I am Captain Mark Daily, Commander of..."

This was more than the King could countenance. "That will be enough! You will only address yourself to me."

To the King's chagrin, Daily's eyes lingered on Elizabeth before he slowly turned his attention to the Henry. "Fine. I am pleased you included most of the influential members of your ruling class here. It makes a lot easier than having to send out numerous proclamations when one will now suffice. As I speak, other members of my forces are taking over the monarchies throughout Europe, including the church in Rome. Each of the rulers has the choice of whether they keep their thrones and titles or not. To do so only requires a complete revision of how you rule your subjects, starting with the end of your cruel feudal system. In return you will receive knowledge that will revolutionize how all live their lives."

As he finished, three armored warriors tried to rush him. They only got a few steps before six quick rounds from the SEALs dropped all three dead to the floor.

"Or we can continue to kill off everyone in this room instead. Any other takers?"

When no one said a word, *King Mark* climbed the steps, stood behind King Henry VII, and put his hand on his shoulder. "Now why don't we clear the room of everyone and get down to business."

The SEAL squad moved to help empty the room, though when the Queen rose to leave, Daily put his other hand out. "I want you to stay to hear what I have to say. You will have a big part in some of the more, shall we say, radical ideas."

The King was about to object, but a firm squeeze to his shoulder stopped him cold. Daily noticed Elizabeth didn't share her husband's consternation, if Daily didn't know better she appeared a little too calm. As much as he tried to shut it down, he sensed an obvious chemistry between him and the Queen.

"This could get complicated real quick," he thought, as he tried to control the testosterone that was coursing through his blood.

Captain Harris of the 160th infantry Regiment of the California National Guard couldn't remember the last time he felt so powerless to keep a situation under control. The Colonel of his Regiment had tasked his unit to help enforce the nightly curfew in place throughout greater Los Angeles.

His area of responsibility was the tony neighborhood of Toluca Lake that straddled the Ventura Freeway along the southern end of the San Fernando Valley and east of the Hollywood Freeway. With all communications down, he couldn't contact the divisional command center set up in downtown Los Angeles. Captain Harris's orders of the day to his men were to double up on the patrols. The film studio personnel that populated the neighborhood were perfectly happy to stay in their upscale homes, that is until all the social networks keeping them informed of their own sense of self-importance went down.

Harris was about to reach for his two-way radio when the useless monitor on his desk flashed to life. "It looks like we're back online." Harris walked over to his desk expecting to see someone from division; instead, he got the punked out Phoenix. "Who are you, and how did you get on our communications link?" Unfortunately for Harris, the signal came in over the emergency broadcasting network, which meant it only went one way.

The video switched to the front of the White House as Aaron Fletcher delivered the narrative by recorded phone conversation. "You've made sure to evacuate all of your essential personnel from the area?"

"Yes we did, and per your advice, we've moved all of our financial assets as well."

Pictures of Aaron Fletcher and the CEO of one of San Francisco's largest financial groups faded in. The date and time of the conversation scrolled at the bottom, one week before the nuclear detonation.

When this conversation ended, another one started, where the date showed three days before. Aaron asked, "Has the package arrived?"

Clearly, the unidentified voice on the other end that responded was military. "Twenty minutes ago, Sir, and has been delivered as ordered." The monitor now showed General Addison, senior commander of America's nuclear arsenal, wrapped in the arms of a woman thirty years his junior, a subject the media had grabbed onto shortly before the crisis began.

Over the next ten minutes more pieces of the conspiracy played out, each in their own right explainable, as an aggregate, overwhelmingly damning.

As the video played on, other soldiers drifted in and watched too stunned to comment until the screen suddenly went dark.

As if on cue, everyone started to talk at once, until Phoenix popped back up. "Sorry to interrupt what I can only imagine was spirited conversation over your leader's treachery, but there is more bad news. This was not only a manipulation of our military's legions of patriotic young warriors, but also a betrayal to their oath of loyalty to protect the Constitution.

"In effect, our beloved military not only became the instrument of a coup, it also stood by while our government attacked the remaining individuals who could offer resistance against the oligarchs complicit in this outrage. They still hide in the shadows competing against one another to see who will ultimately become the next era's version of the Rockefellers and Kochs."

As she continued, pictures of the Kremlin and Beijing flashed behind her. "When the Cold War ended over twenty-five years ago, it was assumed the West won. Who really won? It certainly wasn't capitalism, and it most certainly wasn't socialism. It makes you wonder what Reagan and Gorbachev really discussed during the arms treaty negotiations that led to the end of the Cold War.

"Once new markets in Russia and China opened after the end of the Cold War in 1990, you Baby Boomers out there who had matured into leadership positions quickly learned the greed and avarice tricks of the oligarchs and brought this corrupted business model home. Disco and Studio 54 were bad enough, but then your narcissism destroyed the last vestiges of social responsibility. I would say you are reaping the destruction you sowed and the ignorance you assumed when, as surveys suggest, one out of four Americans believe God created the Earth six thousand years ago, and dinosaurs walked with humans."

Phoenix then ratcheted up her rage. "Unfortunately, you took the rest of us with you. Aaron Fletcher could not have accomplished so much, so quickly without an entire generation's duplicity."

The camera on Phoenix panned back to show the rest of the

group, with Sean Anthony off camera. "Every member of our families and most of our friends have been brutally murdered in an attempt to stop us, so what do you think is going to happen when you are no longer needed?"

A video of President Harrison's casket carried up the Capitol steps replaced the group. "If they can get away with killing a President in the White House Oval Office..." She shrugged and the screen went dead.

Not only did bedlam break out in the small strip mall that Captain Harris called his command center, but also in hundreds of other regimental command centers throughout the United States. Not only did this bomb hit the military at the lowest ranks, the same video with a different voiceover aired exclusively over all the nation's 24-hour news services whether they like it or not. Foreign language versions found their way around the control filters into every country, so within an hour of the initial broadcast any sane person with a phone, tablet, laptop, TV, or radio on the planet knew the truth.

The steps necessary to ignite a rebellion against this tyranny began tentatively at first with a trickle of intrepid souls leaving their homes and walking up to one of the military roadblocks on Ventura Boulevard. With their tablets in hand, they shared the news with the soldiers who hadn't received it. This quickly accelerated to one hundred, then a thousand, until it seemed the entire city was in the streets.

This happened from Los Angeles, to Phoenix, on to Chicago, then all the way to Times Square. Unfortunately, the military units still under direct command of the conspirators maintained their chokehold, and ruthlessly gunned down anyone brave enough to challenge them. These fanatics still controlled Washington, DC, two Air Wings, and most of the southern states. A civil war was a real possibility as the night wore on.

In the cave in China, the hackers released the pent-up energy of the last two days in a wild celebration. Adonis clicked his Red Bull and Vodka filled glass with Phoenix's bottle of water. "There is something about you girl that makes me wish I were fifteen years younger and a hell of a lot smarter."

"You might want to add better looking, sunshine."

The expression on his face mirrored a hurt puppy, until he realized she was messing with him. Phoenix planted a kiss on his cheek. "You're awfully gullible for someone purporting to have street smarts."

"You've been working on that little gem you dropped for some time," Adonis stated as a compliment.

"Do you remember the jamming worm Heart Bleed back in 2014?"

"You used that as your platform?"

"Been working on it for four years, and the information we took from the NSA gave me the final pieces. Apparently they spent much their time trying to figure out and replicate what I did." Phoenix pulled Adonis close, and whispered in his ear. "Wait until we have the time to take a close look at some of the malware we downloaded from their servers. We can keep the government spooks tied up for decades chasing their own creations, and the beauty of it all is they will never know we are there."

"That is a big if." Both of the hackers jumped in surprise that Sean Anthony now stood directly behind them.

Adonis's voice betrayed guilt. "How long you been standing there?"

"Long enough. Why don't you clue the rest of the group into your treasure trove so they can see if there is anything helpful?" Sean Anthony paused before he added, "I've got bigger plans for the two of you."

The next morning at the Vatican, found Alicia wandering in the vastness of the old St. Peter's Basilica with the Gunnery Sergeant in charge of the Marines and Naval personnel attached to the Vatican. Both of them scanned the massive structure from ceiling to floor in silence as they tried to take it all in. Alicia stopped suddenly and waved her arms in the air. "You have to hand it to the Romans; they sure knew how to make a statement.

"Taking communion must have been a bitch," she continued, "serving what looks like could be three or four thousand. This place is easily longer than a football field."

They walked down the wide center aisle, one of five that led to the altar at the front.

Alicia took a moment to stroke one of the twisted granite columns that helped to support the structure. "These are the same columns they used to build the baldachin to cover the new altar when they built the St. Peter's Basilica we know."

The Marine Commander looked at her inquisitively. "Baldachin, ma'am?"

Alicia laughed. "Sorry Gunny, the baldachin is the ornamental canopy over the altar in the new St. Peter's Basilica. I know because I spent a full day as a tourist there ten years ago. I may not like what the church represents, but I do appreciate the genius of the architects and dreamers who engineered the functional works of art that have stood for centuries. This place lasted twelve hundred years, and the Basilica that replaced it will likely do the same."

"All I see is thousands of people listening to some fool threatening them with an eternity in Hell if they don't surrender their souls." The Gunnery Sergeant was obviously speaking from experience.

"Why I never would have taken you for a reformed Catholic, Gunny."

"Yes, ma'am."

Fifteen minutes later, they stood on either side of the Pope, who gazed apprehensively toward the balcony he was about to walk out on.

Alicia gave Pope Alexander a last minute prod. "Think about it Alex, twenty minutes of repudiating everything you stand for, and then you can keep your job."

Down below, the plaza was jammed with thousands of people hoping their spiritual leader could explain the terrifying demons that added more stress to their already dark lives.

With a shove from the Gunnery Sergeant, the Pope stumbled through the door onto the balcony. Alicia listened to his sermon from behind the curtains to make sure the Pope followed the script she had written earlier. When he finished, the masses below remained silent, shocked and most likely very confused at what they heard. Alicia didn't expect anything less, as it would take more than a single speech to turn around centuries of voodoo indoctrination.

As Alicia pondered this, Sean scanned the ocean ahead from the bridge of the Enterprise. With the port of Marseille, France only an hour away, he ordered, "Lt. Layworth, order the CIC to execute Operation France."

"Aye Aye Admiral. Order CIC to execute Operation France."

This time Tony would lead the expedition, and right now he sat next to Commander Thornton in one of the Seahawks tasked to Lyon, the banking and trading center of 15th Century France. The Pope's emissary sat across from them carefully cradling the Pope's proclamation. By now, the 30-year-old priest had overcome his earlier terror of the *demons* once he experienced their humanity. Now here he sat flying like a bird of prey in the sky without any idea of how these incredible people accomplished this miracle. He never felt so alive.

Recognizing Tony's impatience, Thorny gave him something else to think about. "We're losing sunlight and still thirty minutes out. Are you sure we will be able to identify the target?"

Tony rolled his eyes. "You're not thinking 15th Century. There is rich, and then there is poor, dirt poor, like African famines poor. Believe me, we will see the difference."

Sure enough, 25 minutes later, the rolling countryside gave way to the medieval city of Lyon, and true to Tony's prediction, large gothic cathedrals dotted the landscape, dominated by the massive St. Johns. As they flew over the city at 500 feet, the panicked populace reminded Tony of a scene out of a Mel Brooks comedy, where no particular direction is chosen in their attempt to escape the flying demons. He half expected them to turn in unison and flip them off as they flew by.

"There it is." Tony had a perfect view of the Chateaux as he pointed to it. "It's where they do all the trading; think of it as their New York Stock Exchange of 15th Century France."

Thorny keyed his mic. "Captain, after the other choppers dispatch their squads, feel free to land as close to the front door as possible." He then announced to his men, "Same as before. Remember, no casualties if possible, quick and neat. Hopefully they will be too stunned to move like the guards at the Vatican were."

Immediately after discharging their fifteen SEALs, the other three Seahawks took off to provide air cover. One minute later Thorny's Seahawk touched down.

Rather than rush the chateaux, they walked calmly up the travertine marble steps to the main door. Next to Tony walked the interpreter, a no-nonsense looking female Marine who kept the hand not holding the stun gun ready to unsling her rifle. "You ever notice how big the rich and powerful make their doors? I wonder why they do that?"

The interpreter looked at Tony as if he had lost his mind. "Sir?"

Tony stared upward toward the impressive size of the manor. "I mean, look at the size of this place. Same thing where we come from, the rich and their need to build personal palaces like huge oversized loincloths. You think they are compensating for something, Corporal?"

"Don't get me started, Sir. Botox butts?"

They shared a quick laugh before Tony motioned her ahead. "Well, shall we?"

"After you, Sir."

Tony reached the door and pushed it open to reveal a grand hall where one well-attired, extremely nervous gentleman's-gentleman's feet stood glued to the floor.

"This keeps getting funnier and funnier," Tony thought. "Tell him we need to speak to the master of the house, and have him get the rest of the staff front and center."

After she translated, and listened to his response, she turned back to Tony. "He wishes to know who we are, and if we are here do harm to the masters of the castle."

Tony again rolled his eyes, reached into his flak jacket, pulled out a cigar, and lit it. "Negotiate away. I'll wait."

After a rapid-fire exchange, *le majordome* yelled out a command and others slowly entered the room. They all lined up as if for inspection, but before they could finish a door opened from the top of the stairs, and a portly man of little more than five feet tall proudly began to descend. His clothes and carriage identified him as the master of the house.

"Who are you, and why have you invaded my home?" the portly lord indigently demanded. As he got closer, he became more belligerent when he saw the strange way the SEALs were dressed. "If you do not leave immediately, I will see all of you strapped to the Breaking Wheel!" This and many threats followed as the interpreter continued to relay his anger until he arrived chest to chest with Tony, who calmly raised his stun gun and pressed the trigger. "When he gets finished convulsing all over the floor, put him on the couch over there." Tony then looked over the rest of the house staff. "Anyone else?"

Early the next morning, they stood in the city center, the now recovered Lord of the Chateaux sweating profusely at the thought of enduring another lightning attack. Off to the side, the Pope's emissary read aloud the Pope's proclamation to the gathered town folk. Surprisingly to Tony, the diminutive priest enjoyed the experience, as evidenced by the dramatic flairs he added to his delivery.

Throughout the rest of the day, and well into the night the city leaders, and by Tony's demand, representatives from the lower classes, went over what the implications of the proclamation from Rome meant to their future. Only once, when one of the representatives of the King of France made a foolish attempt to attack the interpreter was there a need to deploy the stun gun. The humorous reaction to his flailing body on the floor from the group of those representing the peasants once again affirmed to Tony all he needed to know about who would not be a threat. "Next stop Dijon. Isn't that the place they make Grey Poupon?"

After receiving from the Enterprise, Navy support staff, supplies, and Marines to replace the SEALs, the group of four attack helicopters traveled two hundred miles north to reach the town of Dijon, Burgundy, a place of tremendous wealth and power where Tony and Thorny repeated their success. After another round of replacements, supplies, and much needed rest, the group then flew west to Amboise. After about five minutes in the air, Tony noticed the Marine interpreter sitting across from him obviously wanted to say something. "I can't blame you if you have questions, Corporal; permission to speak freely."

She swallowed hard before answering. "Sir, I am not clear about why, if we are going after the French royalty, we are heading away from Paris."

"Believe me, I would love nothing better than to see what the city looks like in its present form. However, according to Captain Aslan's research, we would find nobody at home in Paris. In medieval times, royalty wanted to live a long healthy life, so it was a good idea to spend as little time as possible around the intrigue that infested the Royal Court in Paris. It wasn't always healthy to be the king. For example, Joan of Arc tried to save the city from the English invaders and what was her reward for duty to King and Country? Betrayal by the merchant class of the city. They burned her at the stake because she threatened the status quo. You see, it was safer to be in the country holed up in a great big castle in a little bitty town like Amboise, than surrounded by pretenders to the throne."

The pilot interrupted Tony's French political lesson. "We've picked up the Loire River, Sir. Twenty minutes out."

Tony looked down and could begin to make out the outlines of the castle they were about to breach. For this mission the cover of darkness, night vision googles, and stealth offered the best chance to keep casualties down, considering the Royal Family had an army posted nearby. Also in his thoughts was the ease in which a small heavily armed and highly trained Special Operations Force could overthrow an entire continent because of the added dimension of fast airborne transportation and assaults against an opponent stuck on a two dimensional battlefield.

Thorny interrupted Tony's thoughts when he announced over the radio to all on the four Seahawks, "Listen up assholes. This is the main event, and the army guarding these people will come after us with a vengeance once we inform them we have the King. Round everybody up, quickly take out anyone who fights back, and get ready for a counter assault. Pretty simple, so let's not screw it up."

"On target." came over the intercom, which prompted the beginning of the exercise. Two SEAL squads rappelled down from two of the Seahawk helicopters onto the parapets of the Château d'Amboise, the residence of King Charles III and his Queen Anne. Another SEAL squad had repelled onto the courtyard. After depositing their fighters, the three Seahawks circled overhead to provide air cover while the Seahawk carrying Tony and Commander Thornton landed outside of the main gate to the compound. As Tony and Thorny disembarked and made their way to the gate, they saw it open before they could reach it.

"We have the King and Queen under control, Sir." The smile on the face of the SEAL who led the attack from the courtyard highlighted that the kid couldn't be more than 20 years old.

Before Tony could take another step toward the gateway, the look on that boy's face turned from a smile, to one of excruciating pain. From behind, six armed palace soldiers had come out of nowhere, and one had shot an arrow into the young SEAL's neck.

Tony didn't have time to think stun gun as he unshouldered his rifle. However, before he could raise it to aim, the six attackers dropped to the ground in rapid succession, the cause of which became clear when he witnessed a bullet slam into the fifth one. Two members of the downed SEAL's squad scanned the area for more hostiles.

Commander Thornton ran up and bent down to discover the young man starred out through dead eyes, which he gently closed. Thorny then strode angrily to the center of the courtyard, and in a commanding voice ordered the strike force, "Check out the lower floors, and this time, make sure there are not any more surprises."

After they walked into the Grand Entry to the Château, Tony angrily shouted to the SEALs on the upper floor, "Take me to *His Majesty*."

"This way, Sir." They led Tony, his interpreter, and Commander Thornton through a long hallway lined with portraits and sculptures of the royal lineage, every one painted or chiseled by a master, until they reached the salon where the SEALs had gathered the inhabitants of the castle.

Aggressively rousted out of a sound sleep, the state of their captives betrayed their normal royal bearing; in fact, they looked more like the hired help. As Tony surveyed the room, he tried to remember from the notes Alicia and Renée had written on the existing French power structure. Five pages of cheat sheets did little to give him direction about how to approach those who believed only God had the right to challenge their authority.

With a nod to his interpreter, Tony addressed the gathering. "I'm not very good with all of your Royal Court manners, so let's start with you, King Charles."

King Charles VIII was easy to pick out of the crowd. Alicia's description was spot on. With an oversized head in relationship to his small body, he looked as if someone had put him together from a set of mismatched parts: oversized mouth, spindly legs, long nose, and feet that looked like they belonged to a Hobbit. Royal inbreeding had not been kind to the monarch's genes.

Charles took a moment to try to figure out what threat these strange looking invaders presented before he answered, "So which of my many enemies do you represent, and what are your intentions?"

Considering his vulnerability, Tony was impressed with the King's outward calm. "Well since you asked so politely, I will tell you. We are here to inform you there are going to be some major changes. This begins with you announcing this proclamation from the Pope in Rome."

As he continued, Tony motioned to the Pope's emissary to show the parchment to the King. "Though you haven't been informed about what has taken place throughout your kingdom, suffice it to say your ability to rule has been seriously reduced. By the way, we discovered your emissaries are not particularly popular among the masses."

Tony watched the King become increasingly upset as the interpreter relayed the bad news. Then suddenly two men of his entourage drew knives and rushed Tony. They only made it halfway to their target before two SEALs triggered their Tasers. As he watched them writhing to the floor, he turned to Commander

Thornton. "This never gets old does it?"

Thorny walked over and ripped the barbs out of both of the incapacitated assailants. With the earlier loss of one of his team, he wasn't in any mood for levity. "Next time it will not be to incapacitate; it will be to kill," Thorny exclaimed loudly as he glared at the two men on the floor, and then glared at everyone in the room to make his point as the Marine Corporal interpreted with the same brusque attitude.

Tony turned his attention back to King Charles. "You know what we want, and you will come to know that you are powerless to contest us either in words or actions. It is very simple, either you work with us and keep your throne, or we turn to your sister Anne, whom I am certain would enjoy resuming her regency."

Tony could see by the King's clenched fists that he had struck a nerve. He could further see there was still hope in his body language, so before he concluded, Tony turned his back to leave, knowing that this was an affront. "Oh, and by the way, if you are counting on your army riding to the rescue, I'll make sure you have a ringside seat when they make the attempt."

Tony smiled as King Charles VIII totally lost it as the interpreter relayed his comments. He assumed by the rage in which the King delivered the words that he was calling the origins of Tony's birth into question.

The next day, once again the Marine units arrived to replace the SEALs, along with Navy support staff and supplies. The day also brought the King's Army that, when met with an awesome show of force from the Seahawks, meekly returned to their encampment while Tony entertained their officers.

Once the French Army was in alignment with the *new old-world order*, Commander Thornton, his SEALs, and the Pope's emissary flew back to the Enterprise near Marseilles for some well-deserved rest. Tony and the Marine interpreter remained to deal with the

Bat Shit Crazy

French Royal Family and the rest of the French nobility.

Communications from Alicia in Rome, Tony in Amboise, and the resourceful Marine commanding officers in Lyons and Dijon proved that they did not need much persuasion to turn the populace against the existing power structure. Changing allegiances and the redrawing of national borders was a way of life in this era. Besides, when you tell a population that they could now keep what they produced and innocent comments would no longer be cause to burn at the stake, the populace spent most of their time celebrating the gods who had come down to Earth. They responded with such an abundance of fresh food and other supplies that they no longer needed to furnish the occupying forces from the task force. Protecting the ruling class from a brutal death at the hands of the formally oppressed peasants could have become their most dangerous job if it wasn't for the gratitude the populace showed toward their saviors.

The Enterprise Task Force now sailed southwest toward their next objective, Valencia, Spain.

———◆———

Phoenix paced the floor of the cave in China like a caged animal waiting for Sean Anthony to reveal what he wanted her and Adonis to work on.

To sell his idea, Sean Anthony knew he needed to wait for her to reach critical mass. He didn't have to wait long.

Phoenix exploded. "I don't know about anyone else, but I am sick of fighting this battle from the shadows. The same sociopaths who worked so long to totally screw up the world are still the power brokers regardless of all that Aaron has done. It's more than past time for us to step forward and use our advanced state of mind to start picking up all the broken pieces. It is time to take a chance, and become part of society again. We should take the battle to them before they figure out how to get their shit together without control of their communications. I imagine they have some old plans dating back to the fifties that they are dusting off."

Sean Anthony wanted her to take the next step without his help. "What's your plan?"

She was prepared, though she loathed what she was about to propose. "As much as I hate to admit this, we need to get the rest of the geeks on our side, and work with them to selectively restore the civilian networks."

Exactly what Sean Anthony wanted to hear. "I know it is difficult for you to admit you need the help, especially from those of your ilk whose morality is measured in dollars, however hundreds of geeks writing code as opposed to...?"

"Wait a minute." Adonis thought of a flaw. "Do you want to expose all of us to the outside world?"

Sean Anthony knew to do so would give Aaron an opportunity to respond. "No reason to endanger everyone, so it will be only you, me, and Phoenix."

"What do you mean only..." was all that Adonis had time to get out before they were gone in the green mist.

Whatever it is about geeks and glass, the headquarters of the world's largest technology giant in computers, cell phones, search engines, and social networking could not have handled one more pane. Under a normal day in this sprawling ego trip to modernism, the working environment would be relaxed with hundreds of One Percenters excited about their new Teslas in the lot, or their stocks reaching a new all-time high. And let's not forget the occasional geek who remained a virgin through high school now announcing his engagement to a model. Yes, they were the Rock Stars of the 21st Century.

However, the last two weeks had been anything but normal, as none of these newly minted multimillionaires had an answer to

Phoenix's malware. Most stressed of all was the founder and CEO of Intelligent Design, Morris Zagruder, who now stared blankly at Sean Anthony, Phoenix, and Adonis who had suddenly appeared seated in his office.

"Yo dawg, you just gonna sit there with that dead look on your mug, or are you going to shout in amazement that three people zapped into here out of nowhere?" Adonis enjoyed watching the discomfort of a man who was used to rubbing shoulders with royalty, not one suddenly confronted by one from the ghetto, and another who looked like she should be texting her BFF.

"Who the hell are you?" Morris jerked out of his frozen state to grab for the intercom to raise the alarm, but remembered like everything else, as part of the computer based phone system connected to the outside world, it no longer worked.

"We are the ones who are going to save your ass." Adonis got up, sat on the corner of the CEO's desk, and smiled. "That is for a price."

The light bulb went off in the CEO's head as he ignored Adonis and stared at Phoenix. "Wait a minute. I recognize you; you're the girl in the video."

Phoenix smiled. "We are much more than that. We are the ones that crashed all of your systems. By now, the billions of people whose lives depended on corporations such as Intelligent Design to sedate their senses, have had time to detox and take a good look around with no one to tell them everything was fine. If you want to keep your multi-billion dollar empire afloat, you might want to listen to what we have to offer."

Considering his entire business would stay in the toilet if he could not find a solution to get back online, his face said it all, "What do you want?"

Five hours later, Morris Zagruder sat in front of a bank of TV cameras in the studio of the CBS affiliate in Silicon Valley with feeds out to the other networks. Ready to read from the teleprompter, he waited as the director counted down and the studio camera's red light lit up.

The graphic behind him began a montage of celebrities for celebrity sake, leading off with the most vacuous of them all, the Kardipians. "Because of the seriousness of the current violence around the world, I will get straight to the point. It should be obvious to anyone with even the most rudimentary knowledge that the state of modern society has reached critical mass, and can no longer support the weight of corruption that drives it.

"We have become a nation of zombie divas, whether claiming to be from the Left or the Right, who have let others brainwash us so only they have a say in what rights and freedoms we can express. As a nation, we are responsible for our current catastrophe. As the founder and CEO of Intelligent Design who provides the tools to maximize the distribution of this mind numbing content, I must shoulder as much of the blame as those who profit from producing and distributing it."

Morris paused for a moment, clearly uncomfortable with what came next. "As the world learned yesterday, the very government you willingly gave away most of your constitutional rights to has proven to be behind one of history's greatest massacres when the late President Susan Harrison ordered the nuclear destruction of San Francisco. With the aid of the nation's military leaders and the complicity of special interest groups who spent the last four decades tearing down the walls of Liberty and Equality, the goal was to silence all dissent with the declaration of martial law and suspension of habeas corpus.

"That this nation's citizens accepted this without any organized resistance, while the military jailed, or worse still, eliminated with extreme prejudice any person of interest, is comparable with the German population's silent acceptance of Adolph Hitler's Night of the Long Knives. For those of you who spend most of your time binge watching your favorite streaming service instead of studying the world around you, this was the Nazi's putsch that not only led to concentration camps, but also the march to the slaughter that was WWII."

For the first time in over twenty years, the insanity he helped to provide slowly dawned on the CEO. His voice quivered as he adlibbed the next portion of his speech. "Think about it. Our government detonated a nuclear weapon in the middle of one of our largest cities, prompting worldwide destruction that at last count has eliminated over 300 million individuals across six continents."

Zagruder glanced to the stage wing to see Phoenix nodding her head to urge him on. "To remedy this lack of the most basic of civic responsibility, beginning today the only information available to the public over all broadcast, cable, and social media networks will consist of a crash course in civics and peaceful civil disobedience.

"Either the world's leaders at all levels will recognize the need to reform the laws that have created a playing field devoid of opportunity for the majority, or they must be replaced by those who can. This means a return to the true interpretation of what our Founding Fathers meant by Freedom, Liberty, and Equality, which must replace the current illogical conservative mantra of small government, toothless regulations, and low taxes. The liberal elites must also realize the need to reign in their reactive collectivism and paranoid compulsion for safety through control.

"Details of the pact between China, Russia, and the United States that clearly dictates our government's plan for the New World Order will replace the daytime soap operas. Details of the Military Industrial Establishment's 70-year stranglehold on the nation's resources will supersede the inane car chases of the evening news. The real state of the modern family will replace silly family sitcoms, and…, well, you get the picture."

The video behind Zagruder changed to show images of military vehicles parked at a city intersection. "To those of you, the brave and confused American soldiers, who were duped into participating in this charade of injustice, help your fellow citizens who have lost the means to feed and supply themselves the disruption of the nation's supply chain has caused."

As Zagruder continued, Sean Anthony slipped away from the confines of the studio to find a window where he smiled when he looked down at the scene in the streets below. Hundreds of people milled about, intermingled with the soldiers who would have earlier ended such a public gathering with extreme prejudice.

Back in the studio, the graphics showed this scene repeated around most of the country. Everywhere except in the southern states, where military units continued to brutally suppress the few who attempted to disobey the government edicts.

Zagruder turned to Phoenix who now sat in the chair next to him. "Next to me you may recognize the individual who broadcast the evidence of the massive government conspiracy yesterday."

Phoenix dove right in. "And one of the people responsible for disrupting your pathetic lives. Personally, I could give a rat's ass if most of you slowly starved to death, especially those of you out there who led the way to divide the nation into factions over the last four decades. Transportation of basic goods and medical emergencies will be the only networks we will release for the immediate future so get used to living like the seventy percent of those whose poverty you so cavalierly dismissed as deserving to suffer.

"To the cable news, radio shows, and the talking heads who spend every 24-hour news cycle with an endless parade of misinformation, misdirection, and flat out lies, your days are over. Consider yourself unemployed, and if you ever show your faces in public again, before doing so, consider I own all of your personal information.

"To the military authorities who have sequestered the United States Congress, as far as I am concerned you can flush them and their corporate masters into the Atlantic Ocean. As of now, there isn't a functioning national government, but worry not because it hasn't functioned for the American public for decades anyway.

"Power for now resides with the people on the street, whether they are freckle-faced 20-year-old soldiers, 50-year-olds with decades of wisdom who the system has cast aside as unemployable and useless, or all of those who the government hasn't locked up or murdered while attempting to fight the good fight. It is now up to all of you whether this nation survives the trials of the next three weeks, or disintegrates into a bloodbath that forever ends our Founding Father's grand experiment.

"To those of you listening, who might be worried that this country is exposed to outside threats, be assured our cyberattacks left them more vulnerable than the United States. Only my group and I have the ability to reactivate the necessary communications links that will allow any military offensive links. We will be in direct communication with the governments who pose the greatest risk to world security very soon. Remember we can activate this nation's nuclear arsenal at a moment's notice, while theirs remain impotent."

Phoenix rose from her chair and stood in front of the desk, a look of total disdain on her face. "Lastly, but most importantly, we are coming for you Aaron Fletcher, and all the military brass you have involved in this travesty. You will pay for San Francisco, for the assassination of President Harrison, though I cry no tears for her timely removal, and most importantly for all the psychopathic horrors you represent."

Sean Anthony had returned and watched from behind the camera. When Phoenix looked in his direction, he mouthed, "The rest is up to you." He gave her a thumbs-up, and turned to Adonis who stood next to him. "Make sure you keep her safe, Bro."

Adonis grabbed his arm. "What's that supposed to mean? You going somewhere?"

"You've got this. I'll see you again soon."

Adonis could only watch as the green mist swallowed Sean

Anthony. At the same time, the green mist deposited all the other geeks from the cave in China right where Sean Anthony had been standing.

While Adonis freaked, Phoenix didn't skip a beat as she witnessed Sean Anthony disappear and the geeks take his place. "One last thing before I leave you to your thoughts. As long as society accepts abuse from those they have chosen to lead them, the government you receive is the government you deserve. The blood of innocents who believed those who promise that to protect you, you must first abrogate your rights is a stain on history. Under pinning these despots has always been the ruling elite whose greed and need to protect themselves from legitimate competition supplied the capital to build the armed forces necessary to enslave.

"Risk and the need to understand the universe around us is intrinsic to the good health of humanity. We are at our best when we attempt the impossible, like sending humans to the moon and building space telescopes that peer back into the very beginnings of time.

"Wake up and feel what it is to live your life looking up and outward instead of face down at your mobile phone. Who knows, you might meet some interesting people along the way. We will be watching, and remember if anything should happen to me or any of my companions, there isn't an individual or group smart enough to undo the coding we've embedded that has paralyzed the modern world."

With that, Phoenix walked off the set over to Adonis and the rest of the geeks. By now, everyone in Sean Anthony's hacker group looked to the 15-year-old with the ancient mind for leadership, though Adonis exercised his unique way in showing it. "Hey little Miss Sassy Pants, what you gonna pull out of your magic Dark Cloud now?"

One seriously pissed off Aaron Fletcher looked over what was left of his former command structure and wanted to kill someone slowly, very slowly and painfully. He could not believe how fast his original foolproof plans had unraveled. He knew from the beginning that if they met any serious opposition, he would lose the Navy. However, he didn't expect General Addison of Strategic Command and General Favors of the Air Force to turn against him when the threat to their survival dictated a hasty political retreat.

Though others were rapidly forming alliances with the civilian community, he couldn't vent his frustrations on all of them without an equal response from Sean Anthony, or worse, so he decided Addison and Favors would have to suffice for now.

General Addison's wife, arms dragging along shopping bags full of Washington's latest fashions, returned home and made her way to the living room. Overburdened to the point she couldn't see the floor ahead, it wasn't until she stepped on something that squished under her foot that she looked down in horror to discover a human lung pinned to the heel of her shoe. Dropping the bags to the ground, she screamed at the sight of a trail of body parts through the house, the last of which was the head of her husband rotating slowly on the BBQ spit.

On the other side of town, General Favor's wife found her husband staked to the ground in his backyard, drawn and quartered. However, neither prey had satiated Aaron's ravenous thirst for revenge.

As Aaron's plans unraveled across the nation, except in the South, which still lay under his control, he knew his hold on the power he needed to finish the job had to shift to a new direction. His exposure as a mass murderer or that he put a bullet in the head of President Harrison, which truth be told was better than the sex he shared with her ever was, didn't bother him. No, his displeasure derived from that he was almost powerless to finish the destruction of this pathetic human experiment. "I need an alternative, and I needed it fast."

While he pondered his limited options, he surveyed the surrounding countryside that was part of Fort Campbell. Unfortunately for Aaron, the massive Army base that straddled the Tennessee and Kentucky border was too isolated to do anything more than threaten St. Louis. Finally, he came up with a plan guaranteed to accomplish his goal. Completely unfazed by the breach in the rules it signified, with a twisted smile the former Chief of Staff to the President of the United States vanished in a flash.

"What's in it for us to risk such folly?" The diminutive grey figure communicated his thoughts clearly without a single movement of his odd shaped face. "The terms of our agreement allow us only minimal interaction with Earth's inhabitants. What you suggest could lead to repercussions of interstellar import."

Aaron had prepared for this line of argument. "What you forget is that Durius has as much right to make changes to this planet's biomass as Darius, so you are covered."

The Grey was skeptical. "If this is so, why would Durius send you to ask for such a favor instead of make the request for such a planetary disruption herself?" Though the representative of the Greys shared Aaron's contempt for the vile human creatures, he wasn't about to take the word of one who had only proven himself a failure. "You carry no weight to make such an agreement."

Aaron chose to ignore the insult. "That would be true if negotiations were not under way for my mother to gain complete authority over the future disposition of this worthless clod of dirt and water."

The Grey scoffed at such an arrangement. "For your own selfish needs you say Darius is incapable of protecting what is his; we on the other hand know better. Our agreement is with him, not Durius; therefore, for us to take the risk to go up against his wishes, you better have something very valuable to exchange for us to do so."

Aaron did his best to suppress a smile. The one important thing to understand when dealing with the Greys was once you could get past their initial risk adverse nature was to make sure you had something they wanted. This was where it got tricky. "How about if I could promise you complete control over this planet, and any other reality associated with it for starters."

This caused the Grey to hesitate before responding. "A Grey colony in this sector of the galaxy? Completely unheard of, and I might add impossible. The agreement we made stipulated any actions we took to procure subjects for our testing must first be approved by either Durius or Darius, and any breach on our part would lead to an outcome disadvantageous to us."

All across the galaxy, the prospect of interlopers controlling even a planet as insignificant as Earth in another's sphere of influence was tantamount to an act of war.

"Once again you fail to remember that once you agree to do so, any responsibility will fall on Durius. Regardless of how Darius will feel about it, he would have to honor it." At this point Aaron would have said anything to get the Grey to commit.

Aaron had one more card to play. "However, if they disappeared from the record, it would prove rather profitable for those who speculated on their demise as sooner rather than later."

Most of the alien abductions, UFO sightings and unexplained phenomenon carried out over the centuries occurred strictly for the purpose of entertaining out of this world guests. Unknown to humanity, gambling afflicted most alien cultures to the same extent as their own addiction. Thousands of humans went missing simply to determine what an individual's reaction to the many forms of torture meted out, and who guessed correctly what they would be. The timing of humanity's destruction was the bet to end all bets.

Though Aaron didn't know it, his desperation played perfectly into this particular Grey's motive. "With the nuclear fallout from your failed efforts, and the years of chaos it will take to bring about any sense of order, your father will not be in a very forgiving mood if we prematurely intercede on your behalf. Though on the other hand, it does look as if the game has played itself out – dull, very dull. However, I think an arrangement can be made, but first you must understand that this entire agreement will be exposed the minute we feel it would be advantageous for us to do so."

Aaron had guessed correctly that this particular Grey could benefit, and so any threat to expose his part in it was inconsequential to him. All that mattered was that for the first time one of his bets was about to pay off.

"Now if only these morons don't take forever to decide when," Aaron thought.

"I don't see how insulting us will make us move any faster." The Grey had read his thought. Fortunately, fate was on Aaron's side because the sooner the Greys acted the better for him. "Tomorrow soon enough?"

Darius [Carl Eddington] motioned for another card from the Black Jack dealer, who then flipped it.

"Black Jack," the gorgeous brunet called out with a sultry drawl.

Darius smiled back, and continued to watch as the rest of the hands played out.

A familiar voice from behind interrupted his thoughts. "Wow Darius, I figured you would more likely be hanging out with your whore, not this clip joint."

Darius didn't bother to turn around. "I was wondering when you would finally show up, Durius. You either must think the end is nigh, or have discovered that Aaron has run into complications only mommy can bail him out of."

"No, it's just that I never get tired of your misguided attempts to immortalize yourself through your pathetic creations, though I have to admit, I didn't see your latest ones becoming extinct so quickly. Usually your little pets stick around longer, like at least two hundred fifty million years longer. Only twenty-seven thousand years? How sad for you."

When Durius sat down in the empty chair next to Darius, her countenance brought a chill to the table, as if a cold front suddenly invaded the room and dropped the temperature 40 degrees. What struck the dealer, beyond the frigid air, were the odd verbal exchanges between the two. "How do you two know each other?"

Darius took a drink from his glass and waved it in front of Durius. "She's my *ex*-wife."

"Kiss ass. You know I hate it when you brag about me."

Durius then gave the dealer a wicked grin, stuck her tongue out, and swirled it around her lips. "Do you want to find out how evil a pissed off ex can be?"

As the Black Jack dealer recoiled and frantically searched for the pit boss, the casino abruptly disappeared, replaced by a deserted stretch of beach on one of the thousands of islands that dotted the South Pacific.

"You do love to take all the fun out of living." Darius looked at her sour expression for any sign that she could be mollified, and though there was nothing, he decided to give it one more shot. "Last time you arrived unannounced they dropped the first atomic bomb. Why don't we let things play out from the sidelines for a change without your usual need for bloodletting?"

"Like you said, I am just no fun. *Anyway*, I am not here to torture you. It has come to my considerable attention that all along it was your intent to set all of this in motion to annoy me further. How else can you explain your inexcusable decision to involve your whore of a girlfriend in the outcome?" Durius snarled, as a Green Lizard drink materialized in her hand. "You of all self-absorbed creatures should know the lunacy of such an arrangement. And I simply can't fathom how you deal with the constant prattling they are *sooo* prone to."

Durius downed the drink before she continued. "I wouldn't have minded so much if you had hooked up with thousands of nubile beauties who would rock your world. Use once and flush. But no – you felt the need to humiliate me instead."

Darius didn't let the contempt he felt show, and instead he calmly countered, "Even if this is true, it would pale in comparison to the destruction you have meted out thousands of times across the realities you have access to. That they give you so much freedom to interfere in such a brutal manner, only highlights the fear our kind have of other species evolving to the point they could conceivably threaten our cozy little existence. We can't have our creations become greater than their creators now, can we?"

"Only because most don't see the value in allowing these humans, as you call them, to exist, ergo the rules are stacked in my favor. You know evil is the best role, and if you were to be honest, you have practiced every one of the same evil qualities you so recently claim to abhor. You have become like a starry-eyed, born-again Christian or someone who just quit smoking – insufferable to all around them."

As Durius talked, they now shifted onto a war torn street where a bomb had gone off and torn apart dozens of bystanders, which could have been one of many that were a daily occurrence across the planet. The mutilated bodies of men, women, and children lay strewn about the avenue like so much garbage. "I still don't understand your affection for these barbaric mutants, but I have to admit they were a lot of fun to mess with, especially the ones who believe they have all the answers. That fellow Hitler was priceless. That was truly over too soon, thanks to your intervening in Stalingrad, Normandy, and especially Midway. And no one noticed something odd about how that sea battle turned out?"

This time a Rusty Nail materialized in her hand. "Let's face it Darius, when given the choice, they are no different than you, in that you can never get enough of it. That is what you get when you cross an advanced civilization with a primitive humanoid that lacks even the most basic empathy for one another, and the proof is in the carnage."

Durius shot the drink down, picked up a rifle that lay next to one of the corpses, raised it to her shoulder, and fired a round into one of the surrounding windows, striking a terrified 6-year-old girl in the head killing her instantly.

"God, I could eat this shit up all day!" Durius dropped the gun and faced Darius. "Seriously *honey*, I couldn't be more pleased.

"I'm sorry, I take that back. I will be more pleased when I tear that little whore of a creature you bed into billions of bloody pieces, all while she is still conscious enough to experience every drop of terror imaginable. You can't keep her away from me forever."

Darius ignored his ex while he repaired the 6-year-old's head wound and whisked her away to St. Jude Children's Research Hospital in Los Angeles. The shocked nurse who witnessed the sudden appearance of the child in the Emergency Room rushed to her side while yelling for a crash cart. Minutes later the young girl, who had watched one of Assad's barrel bombs wipe out her entire family, was well on her way to a better life. Darius ate *that* shit up.

He then smiled at Durius. "Who said anything about hiding her from you?"

The Spanish port city of Valencia was in the middle of a Golden Age where culture, art, and again most importantly, trade and banking flourished. However, as in their other sudden appearances across the Mediterranean, when the massive silhouette of the Enterprise appeared on the horizon, many of the populace scattered to escape the otherworldly apparition.

This time it was Renée's turn to act as ambassador for the group, as she spoke fluent Spanish.

Sean and Rebecca rode the plane elevator down to the ladder with her where three launches waited bobbing on the water below. Renée had misgivings when she realized how small the force was that Sean thought she needed to accompany her on her mission.

"You think thirty SEALs are enough?"

"So far that has been the magic number, besides I've given you an added force multiplier in Commander Thornton to keep you safe. Remember, most of those in town are looking at us as either gods or agents of the Devil. So, the sooner we show up and everybody lives, the less chance the church can succeed in condemning us as the later." Sean took a chance at humor. "Besides, of all the people I could send, you have died, so who's to say you aren't a goddess?"

With a look best described, as *you have to be kidding me*, Renée shot back, "I expect that comment from Tony, but you? Alicia is right; you are becoming more like him."

Rebecca also sent a look of disapproval Sean's way before giving Renée a quick hug. "Good luck. At least you get to step on dry land."

The now fully rested and recovered scientist gave Renée a kiss, and turned to head back to monitoring Specter, which, since Carl had disappeared, became one of the most boring tasks on the ship. Rebecca felt sorry for herself over Carl's absence as she walked slowly across the hangar bay. However, she cheered up considerably when she saw the first wisps of green mist appear around her as she stepped through the door to Specter's operations room. "This better be good."

Twenty minutes after Renée, Commander Thornton, and the Pope's emissary departed the Enterprise in the launch and steered for the docks of Valencia, a Seahawk touched down on the Enterprise flight deck. Sean smiled as Alicia stepped out of the side door and headed over to him. After a brief hug, they made their way back to their quarters.

After they arrived, Sean poured them both a drink and headed over to sit on the couch. "So how was your day?"

Alicia played along. "Oh you know, like any other where you establish a form of government on a population clueless about how to self-govern. And yours?"

"Tony and the Marine commanding officers pretty much report the same. Commander Thornton did complain upon his return about Tony being a little too comfortable in the deity role. He thinks he probably became too accustomed to the Taíno worshiping him."

Sean noticed Alicia wasn't paying attention, so after he repeated the last sentence to no response, he added, "So I thought it might be okay with you if I shacked up with Rebecca tonight."

"Shacked up with who?"

"I can't think a single time since we have been together that I remember you so distracted. What's up?"

"I don't know. It's just…"

Something was obviously bothering his wife and it being an extreme rarity that she would have trouble giving voice to a concern, Sean decided his best option was to wait. He didn't have to wait long.

"Doesn't it bother you that everything is going our way all of a sudden? One minute the sky is full of missiles and nuclear weapons aimed at us, the next it is perfectly all right to take over the known world. Seriously, I don't understand any of the logic about what we are doing. Where did the conflict go?"

As if right on cue, the phone interrupted. "Spooky, isn't it?" She reached over and picked it up. After she listened for a moment, she handed the phone to Sean. "It's Forrest. He wants to know if you have seen Rebecca."

"She was headed back to Specter after Renée left about half an hour ago." As Sean listened, the lines deepened on his face. "It's a big ship Dr. Phelps; I imagine she is walking around trying to figure out how to make computers that can procreate, or flirting with some sailor." After he hung up, Sean called the Master-At-Arms on duty and ordered her to perform a ship wide search for Rebecca.

Alicia figured Sean's glib response was obviously for Phelps's benefit. "So you do think something is up."

"It's probably nothing," Sean said hopefully, as he hung up the phone.

"Yeah, like it's always nothing, just as I was complaining about everything becoming so easy." Alicia started to rise from the couch when she noticed the telltale green mist begin to rise from the deck. "Yep, really nothing at all."

The next moment Sean and Alicia found themselves seated in the most elaborate room either had ever seen. Based on the tapestry draped elevated throne that stood against the far wall, they were about to be introduced to royalty. Unfortunately, the man seated on the throne was anything but a medieval king. His position on the throne was less than regal, as he sat sideways with one leg draped over one of the ornate arms, a branch of grapes dangling from his left hand.

"Welcome to Isabella and Ferdinand's throne room in Alcazar Castle, right here in beautiful downtown Segovia. Sorry the King and Queen are a little tied up right now, however after we have our little chat, I will be more than happy to introduce you to what is left of them." He ripped a huge bite out of the bunch of grapes. "When in Rome."

The detail in the room was stunning, as every square inch had the touch of a master artisan etched into it. Sean looked at Alicia, and they both nodded their heads in agreement. "Okay, are you part of Franklin and Bowie's team, or are you one of those shadowy figures we are meant to help vanquish?" The relaxed tone in Sean's voice conveyed a dismissal of the man being a threat.

"I guess I shouldn't be surprised after all the adventures you both have seen and been a part of. Events that should never have happened to you, yet here we are. Excuse me for my bad manners. I am Aaron Fletcher, and I represent the absolute worst instincts of human nature. The Lindberg baby? Yes, that was me. The man needed to learn some humility, and after all wasn't I correct, him being such a big fan of Adolph. However, listen to me bragging about another's lack of humility."

Then displaying a sense of danger, he added, "Let's discuss yours."

"Only a fool would suggest they lacked humility." Alicia attempted to draw Aaron out. "I can assure you, both Sean and I remember every mistake we've made in that department."

"True, however there are many departments you both are completely oblivious to, and I am here to show you them all." With that, Aaron disappeared, only to reappear right between Sean and Alicia. He quickly tapped them on the forehead, and the sparks began to fly.

Without warning, they found themselves side by side in the castle dungeon, chained to a rough-hewn wall. Aaron stood once again between them. "Remember them?" He turned a mirror he now held to show them. A bruised and battered Isabella stared back at Alicia, while Ferdinand shared Sean's face.

These were not the only images Sean had to quickly associate as Aaron forced him to look back through his lineage. Not only were there an abundance of benevolent leaders, prophets, and architects, there were also some of the most despised individuals in history. "Oh my God, I built the Parthenon, was party to the pyramids, and the Roman aqueducts," roared like a freight train through his brain.

Then a cold blast of brutal psychopaths replaced the memories of accomplishment with those of horrific slaughter that he had ordered and participated in with relish. From Attila the Hun to Pol Pot and Josef Stalin, Sean found it difficult to look at Alicia, and he felt like his ability to maintain his mental equilibrium was quickly breaking to pieces.

Then out of the shadows, a new image began to take shape, one where a new memory metabolized around his love for Alicia. Alicia's love flowed through him like a shot of adrenaline, along with words of encouragement to stomp down the evil he obviously had wrecked on others. As one, they turned to face their tormentor.

Alicia spoke for them. "So now that you exposed who we are, what do you hope to accomplish by keeping us chained in this dungeon?"

"I am curious to find out which aspect of your essence would win if put under a life or death choice." Aaron paused to pick up a sharp metal iron with a pair of tongs from out of a cauldron of burning coals. The instrument of torture radiated red hot at its tip. He slowly raised it to within inches of Alicia's breast. "Any thoughts?"

A terrified Sean fought to maintain his composure, but Alicia interceded within their shared state of mind. "Don't worry lover. He can't hurt us. This too shall pass." To drive her point home, she opened the moment Joan of Arc felt the first flames lick her ankles.

Aaron drove the rod deep into the side of her breast, which immediately drove both bodies to flail helplessly in agony. He just as quickly withdrew it from the deep wound, the heat of the poker cauterizing it so not even a trickle of blood formed on the singed blouse.

"Come on. Where is that monster Pol Pot. Can I have some Attila with a side of Vlad the Impaler, please?" Aaron carefully placed the poker back in the cauldron.

"Focus on her faith." Alicia struggled to keep hold of Joan's belief she served a higher purpose, and shared it with Sean. As the flames from her pyre now roared up her body they both went numb, so when Aaron picked up the poker and applied it to Sean's genitalia, they felt nothing.

A split second later Sean and Alicia found themselves back in the throne room in their own bodies, both severely shaken, but physically unharmed. Aaron once again sat on the throne, the poker still in his hand.

"Not bad for your first go around. Too bad for the King and Queen though. How do you feel about their sacrifice?"

"Go to Hell, whoever you claim to be." Thanks to Alicia, Sean had quickly regained control. "From the bits and pieces I've picked up as a party to this game, you definitely are coloring outside of the lines. In fact, I am willing to bet your being here is a move of desperation because you got your ass kicked somewhere else." Then with either clever insight, or blind luck, Sean added, "My guess is Carl was responsible for your good old fashioned down home ass whooping."

This sent Aaron into a rage. Without a word, Sean and Alicia found themselves in the middle of a medieval battlefield on horseback. They arrived at the Battle of Hastings, where the Norman forces of William the Conqueror had surrounded the doomed King Harold II. Gruesome slaughter quickly ensued, with Sean and Alicia feeling all of Harold's fear as they watched the guards around him disintegrate under the onslaught leaving the King defenseless. It then only took seconds for his attackers in their bloodlust to hack him apart beyond recognition with Sean and Alicia feeling every slice.

This was only the first of over 100 horrible deaths they would experience in rapid succession, and without a single moment to register the horror or give each other comfort.

What they did have time for between these scenes of the macabre was to reach out to the thousands of other personalities Aaron's awakening had stirred up in them. for. Through the brutality, Sean was first to feel the one who, except for Aaron's reality jump transgression, should not be there nibbling at the edges of their consciousness. Then with all the remaining energy they could summon, it happened.

Sean and Alicia collapsed onto the couch in the Admirals Ready Room on the Enterprise, trembling as they tried to untangle their minds from the mental onslaught Aaron had put them through.

"I'm sorry you had to experience all of that," Sean Anthony

apologized, as he stood in the middle of their quarters.

Sean tried to manage a smile as he caught his breath. "Who the hell was that, and who, or what are you?"

"That, my friends, was Aaron, son of Durius, and his actions are partially responsible for all the craziness you are squarely in the middle of. He is one of those who have worked so hard to end humanity's existence."

Sean Anthony walked over to the bar and poured three glasses of Jack Daniels Single Barrel, and after he handed one each to Sean and Alicia, he leaned down and tapped their foreheads. "So now you know my connection to Aaron, though I'm sorry that I can't open all the doors into who and what I represent. That can only happen if we are still around when this is over."

As Sean began to recover, he felt his entanglement with Alicia slowly recede, the both of them sorry to see it end. With the loss, Sean refocused his attention on his ability to command. "So what happens next? Are the King and Queen dead? Or was that Aaron implanting false images in our heads to torture us, and if so to what end?"

"Did the history you shared with Alicia feel fake? I think not." Sean Anthony raised his index finger to make the number one. "First off, all that you experienced while under Aaron's control was real, so yes Isabella and Ferdinand are dead, which complicates your mission here as you will take the blame. You knew the Spanish Army would ride to the rescue of their royals, but all you had to do was trot them out to announce the Pope's decree. With them dead, not so much. The Spanish Army will be out for blood regardless of their chances, so you need to act, though on the bright side, Aaron's intrusion gives you some leeway in how you meet the challenge."

Alicia connected the dots. "When you say we have some leeway, does that explain why you are able to be here as a tit for tat? And would that also explain why two obviously powerful entities decided to grace us with their appearances from out of nowhere.

If I were a betting person, I would speculate that you have more in common with our Mr. Bowie and Franklin than you are willing to admit."

Sean took it from there. "And if this is true, then your psychopathic counterpart is the one that kept sending those who attacked us. Then if you factor in that we are only playing a part in your drama, you two must be very busy blowing up other realities. This of course leads to the question of how many different scenarios are in play, and how many others you have put in the same position as us."

Sean Anthony smiled, understanding why his mother liked these two. They were special. "Or maybe you should be more concerned with how you plan to keep a nation of seven million Spaniards from eventually figuring out they can overwhelm your limited resources. As to why Aaron wanted to kill you, all I can say is he is very frustrated, and he has never learned how to accept failure. The long game has never been his strong suit."

Though Alicia knew from their previous encounters with Carl by way of Rebecca that it would be impossible to get the complete story, she had to ask. "Could you at least for the sake of a little sanity explain what Franklin and Bowie represent in all of this?"

"Would have rather been dropped into your current situation without anyone around to help guide you through it? Think of them as godparents whose only concern is to make sure you survive until you can learn to take your first steps."

Sean Anthony's analogy didn't sit well with Sean. "So now we are just babies learning how to walk?" As soon as he said it, Sean realized his mistake.

Sean Anthony smiled. "Exactly. How can a species that spends most of its time destroying everything around it be considered anything more than a petulant child?"

"And you are supposed to be the adult in the room?"

Sean Anthony ignored Alicia's dig. "By the way, he will not be a threat to you any longer. He just left, which means it is time for me to go as well."

The mist began to appear, but Alicia tried to get one last mystery solved. "Where is your mother, and is she all right?"

Sean Anthony smiled, pleased that she figured out who he was. "She is with dad, and they are both extremely well thank you," he answered as he disappeared.

Sean had no idea who Sean Anthony was. "How did you know?"

"He has his mother's eyes, and the way he talked reminded me of her. You know, a women's instinct."

With his sudden disappearance, all the stress they experienced over the last few hours overloaded their emotions. Alicia was first to crack as tears began to flow unchecked down her face. Sean lost it after he took her in his arms to comfort her. For the next five minutes, they sat swaying back and forth in each other's arms. Sean gently cupped her face in his hands and gave her a tender kiss. Much to his surprise, she aggressively attacked his mouth, and in a mounting frenzy ripped her blouse wide open. They staggered their way into the bedroom where they spent the rest of the day performing acts banned in all the Middle Eastern nations.

Though still traumatized, as they lay naked on their bed, their now exhausted state allowed them the time to refocus on the matter at hand.

Alicia sat up and tried to straighten out her hair. "CIC time."

Though it was the last thing he wanted to do, Sean stood up and began to dress. "You take me to all the nicest places."

Once they were presentable, he grabbed her hand and off they went.

———✦———

As the green mist enveloped her body, the view of the Specter control room disappeared, replaced by the living room in the house Rebecca recognized as her home in Guantanamo Bay, Cuba when Sean Anthony was in first grade.

Carl appeared from the kitchen wiping his hands on a towel and smiling as he asked as if it was just another day, "So, did you bring us anything for dinner?"

"What do you mean, did I bring anything?" Rebecca burst out. "What in the hell is going on?"

Before Carl could respond, a mature version of Sean Anthony walked through the front door.

Rebecca rushed over and gave him the hug to end all hugs. "I missed you so much."

After she released her hold on Sean Anthony, Rebecca slapped Carl hard across the face. "You two have very little time to explain yourselves before I lose it completely."

"I think this is between you and dad, so I am going to check on dinner."

Rebecca ignored her son and fixed her gaze on Carl. "I am waiting. Spill it."

"As of right now, we are in the year 2018 in the 1940s reality we saved from WWII. Sean Anthony and Phoenix have done a wonderful job of continuing the work you and I stared before we left in 1951."

"So where is Phoenix? Please tell me she is out running errands and will be here shortly."

Carl shook his head no. "She is still in the middle of wrapping up some important work. She'll return when she finishes."

Carl took his reluctant wife in his arms. "For you to understand let me show you your lineage."

Rebecca nodded okay, but asked, "Can you promise me one thing?"

"What's that?"

"If it doesn't feel right, you will wipe it all away if I tell you too."

"Agreed." Carl put his lips to hers, and Rebecca immediately became aware of all who she had been.

"Oh my God!" Rebecca soared through the millions of other memories she shared with the past and present, and each time found Carl was there with her. "You caught up with me each time. Why did you keep this away from me through so many centuries?

God, it must have sucked being Romeo."

"You have no idea." Carl kissed her again, this time with more meaning.

Within her expanded awareness, a light bulb went off in Rebecca's mind. "So how many lineages were eliminated to achieve this ideal world?" Then another thought, less wonderful, more curiosity, flashed across her overloaded synapses. "Is it over?"

Carl took a deep breath of relief and let it out. "To answer your second question, answers the first. It is not over, and the outcome of the lineages is still in question. The other two realities have not been decided yet, and are not in time alignment with ours yet. We have two weeks at most until we know if any of it will remain in existence or not."

Rebecca smiled up at her soul mate. "If it has to end, it was an incredible ride," Rebecca sighed, as she leaned into Carl before they walked arm in arm to join Sean Anthony in the kitchen.

———⊰❖⊱———

When they stepped through the door to leave the studio, Phoenix and Adonis found themselves in the middle of a crush of humanity. What passed as the modern media lead the mob, complete with trampling on anyone who got in their way.

"Holy shit! Where did all of these reporters come from?" That was as far as Adonis got, as a hundred flashes blinded them both. Before either could react, the mob's sheer weight of numbers forced them back into the building. A semicircle developed like predators cornering their prey right before the lunge for the throat.

"How did you learn about the conspiracy? What role did you play? How do we know it wasn't you? Were you in a romantic relationship with the former Chief of...?" The questions were shot like pellets from a scattergun, each missile hitting home, and try as Adonis might, he found it impossible to shelter Phoenix from the onslaught.

The thought that under the cover of the media crush, someone in the crowd might have motives more sinister suddenly occurred to Phoenix. They had to get away. "For those of you from the media who insist on invading our space, we will not waste a second of our lives humoring your vacuous speculations. In case you haven't noticed, out of all the targets on Aaron Fletcher's hit list, not one of you was on it. That is a pretty sad commentary on the whole sorry lot of you, if you ask me."

As Phoenix hoped, the swarm of lemmings stopped for a moment to think. She then pushed Adonis hard ahead of her before they could regroup. "Run, you stupid goliath!"

With Adonis as a blocker, they burst through the ring of reporters, only to find another mass outside when they reached the street. "Shit."

Just when they thought the mob closing from both directions would crush them, a female voice amplified by a loudspeaker broke through the crowd's noise. "Clear the area immediately. Anyone who doesn't leave will be viewed as an enemy combatant, and dealt with accordingly."

Everyone, including Phoenix and Adonis froze in silence, until the armored vehicle with the loudspeaker, followed by a convoy of other military vehicles parted the crowd. Then mayhem ensued, as the people on the street knew from their previous experiences with the Army over the last few weeks that live ammo would soon follow.

The only one not moving was Phoenix. Adonis had made it only a few steps when he realized she was not following. "What are you waiting for, girl? Big old nasty soldiers with badass guns, so now is not the time to freeze up on me."

"We're not going anywhere. People have to know to stand up, or everything we did is a waste of time." She planted her feet, and defiantly crossed her arms.

Adonis looked at her, and looked back at the closing soldiers in full body armor, and like he said, armed with badass guns. "Ah

shit, I knew you would be the death of me the minute I saw you."
He stepped back and stood next to her, striking a mirror pose.

Except for the rapidly approaching soldiers, amazingly Phoenix
and Adonis found themselves to be the only people left on the street.
Ten yards short of the two defiant hackers, the soldiers spread out
to take up defensive positions around them facing outward. Then,
as a further surprise, the one closest to Phoenix gave her a wink
before he too turned away.

Adonis shrugged his shoulders. "I didn't see this coming, did
you?"

"Settle down tiger. We still don't know their intentions."

"Our intentions are to see you safely from the area, Miss Phoenix."
The eagle epaulets on her collar identified the 40-something soldier
as a Colonel, and obviously the one in command.

Phoenix remained defiant. "How do we know we can trust you?"

"How about that you're still standing, and the mob that was
about to trample you is gone, except those." The Colonel pointed
back to the reporters taking pictures through the windows from
inside the building. "Shall I order my command to shoot them for
you?"

Phoenix was about to object, when the stern demeanor of the
Colonel relaxed into a smile. "That's okay. A more just sentence
would be to make them all watch network news from the sixties
until it drives them to kill themselves."

They walked over to her command car, but before Adonis got in,
he looked back over to the reporters. "Yeah, and any who don't off
themselves, you can kill."

As the vehicle accelerated, in a blast of guilt Phoenix yelled out,
"Stop!"

The young private driving looked at the Colonel for orders. She
shook her head no, and turned to Phoenix. "What is it?"

"Our friends are still trapped back in the studio."

For the second time, the Colonel smiled. "No, they're not. I had a second team take them out the back while we rescued you. They will meet us at the safe house I have set up. The name's Colonel Valerie Brighten."

Fortunately for Phoenix and her team, the Colonel happened to be one of the good ones. After she had watched the broadcast from a few blocks away she convinced those under her command that their priority was to protect the geeks. She decided the safest place to take them would be to her headquarters at the Carlson Hotel with two acres of empty field on one side, and close to the highway on the other. She had taken the precaution to put the entire hotel on lockdown, and stationed twenty-five soldiers throughout the building as an added security detail.

In a room Colonel Brighten allocated for them in the sub-basement, the geeks began to set up the equipment they had requisitioned from the studio. The now cramped room left just enough space for the pop tart toaster, boxes of Trix, Velveta, bread, and a refrigerator full of the Red Bull and Vodka that Adonis immediately went for.

"Isn't it amazing how the only topic of interest Zagruder concerned himself with was how soon we would allow the net to be brought back up?" Adonis observed.

Phoenix had to get past the disgust of watching Adonis take a drink of his Red Bull & Vodka to chase down the Trix before she answered sarcastically, "Think it might have something to do with the billions the hedge funds and investment bankers can't access with it being down?"

Adonis added his take. "Then there are the gamers, social media addicts, anyone with a cell phone, and all the poor drug addicts and their suppliers who have lost their whole purpose for living. Thank God I kept my iPod, or I might be panicking with the rest of them."

Phoenix punched his shoulder. "What are you talking about? Considering we are still able to connect whenever we want, not the same thang, dawg."

Adonis winced. "What I want is for you to stop punching me every time you don't agree with me."

Phoenix reached out a hand to rub where she hit him, but he grabbed it, and with his other hand tried to force-feed a spoonful of his Trix. This led to a five-minute free-for-all that ended with them rolling on the floor in laughter, Red Bull, Trix, and sticky milk all over them and the carpet.

From then on out, the team focused on setting up the equipment, and relaying to Colonel Brighten other pieces of equipment they still needed to finish their mission. This included servers, studio cameras, and enough audio gear to fill the adjoining five rooms.

By ten o'clock the next morning, they had re-established direct communications with most of the governments of the world.

"Are you sure this is a good idea?" Adonis was alone with Phoenix ten minutes before she was to take the next step. "Think about it. You, a blue-eyed blonde girl who looks more like someone pledging at some Ivy League sorority, are about to dictate terms to the monsters who are in charge of most of the world's population. And need I remind you that some of those monsters have been lobbing thermonuclear weapons around like Frisbees. Maybe this calls for someone a little more mean and nasty."

Phoenix laughed. "You do know the world we hope to build will be color and gender blind, but I do believe you are aware that this is not the world we are now talking to. If cute and menacing doesn't handle it, then we can hit them with the Black Panther."

"The Black Panther; I like the sound of that."

"Good, now can we get on with it?"

Adonis smiled and nodded yes.

After the marathon of sometimes very tense communications that lasted until early the next morning, Phoenix and Adonis fell into their beds in the Carlson penthouse and slept for ten hours, oblivious to the revolution her demands had instigated.

Without the ability to fire the power stations to provide electricity to the urban centers, a pleasant side effect came about. For the first time in over a century, the air quality throughout the world dramatically improved. Though the needs of the major urban centers still lagged behind supplies, the number of civilian casualties dropped as the citizens of the world banded together in small groups, and rediscovered the joys of face-to-face communication while helping each other.

When they awakened, Phoenix and Adonis joined Colonel Brighten at the dining room table in their suite at the Carlson for a very late brunch.

Phoenix was pleased after reading the results the rest of the team put together while they slept. "With China, Russia, and India standing down their forces, we can send out patches to get elements of their communications back up. However, to be safe, we'll keep their missile codes locked out."

With the only comm links available to the military in her hands, Colonel Brighten had made good use of the last ten hours as well. "While you slept, elements from numerous Army units have converged in the area in support of your actions, and two carrier strike forces are stationed off the coast. Several squadrons of F-35s and F-18s out of Lemoore Naval Air Station and Travis Air Force Base have repositioned to Moffett just north of us. They are now flying cap over a 250 mile area around us."

The Colonel's Communications Officer and her media adjunct entered the suite and handed her a communique that she read and then nodded her approval before turning back to Phoenix and Adonis. "Fortunately, it looks like most of the armed forces in the region are coming here to support you, but I had to turn away many other units because of the lack of logistics to support them. Also, you should know your friends are still working downstairs, and it seems they have most of the best coders around the world helping.

"Then there is the rumor spreading about your romantic relationship with Adonis. How do you wish to deal with that?" This news came from the Colonel's media adjunct who, based on the look on Phoenix's face, now wished she hadn't brought it up.

Adonis almost spit out the cereal in his mouth. "Sweet. Can't do anything but raise my street cred." He pursed his lips to further mock Phoenix. Bad move.

"What are you on about?" Phoenix reached over to wipe his chin before she realized where this was going. "What? Like you and I hooked up? That's sick. Hold on, why would you care what anyone thinks?" she added with suspicion. She instinctively knew there was something else bothering him. "Spit it out."

"You do remember Sean Anthony told us something bad has to happen soon before he went poof on us."

Phoenix could see by the look on Adonis's face that he was on a much different track. "What does that have to do with you and me?"

Adonis feigned shock. "It pisses me off people would think because I'm black and you're white..."

Phoenix didn't let him finish. "When did you start trying to sound like an old pervert? I'll bet you..."

Phoenix was in turn interrupted, her mouth opened in shock when Franklin and Bowie suddenly appeared in a green flash standing next to the equally surprised Adonis, the Colonel, and the rest of her staff.

"Who let you two freaks in?" Adonis jumped up from the dinner table to place himself between them and Phoenix, who stood up behind him ready for action.

A glass of wine appeared in Franklin's hand, while a lit joint materialized between Bowie's fingers, from which he then took a swift hit. "Down tiger. We are not here to harm either of you. We're the cavalry luv, tasked with keeping your fairy tale dream alive."

Looking with disdain at Adonis, Bowie then added, "Not so

much hope for you. It seems you received a mix of the carnal aspect into your lineage."

Phoenix ignored the dig at Adonis's moral character as she stepped to his side. "So where exactly are your horses tied up?"

"Oh, isn't she the clever one; cavalry, horses, I get it." Franklin took a sip from his glass before he continued. "How about this for a start. Mr. Aaron Fletcher has met with his other worldly sources to drop a bomb on your parade."

"What bomb?" Phoenix detected seriousness beneath the stranger's jocular nature.

Unfazed by the sudden appearance or the incongruity of the two characters, Colonel Brighten wasn't buying any of it. "Though he can access the nuclear weapons in the South, he lacks the ability to launch. These two helped make that impossible. He could try transporting them by land, but we can track any military movement by both satellite and the surveillance cameras the NSA was kind enough to string together for us. Besides, our quarantine of the remaining military units under his control makes it impossible to launch coordinated strikes of any type. We see everything they do, while they are completely blind on land and in the air. Also, the Navy is completely with us."

Impressed by the Colonel's commanding presence, Bowie bowed down. "How did a lowly Colonel manage to put all of that together so quickly?"

"Can I shoot him?" Colonel Brighten asked Phoenix, only half kidding.

Franklin quickly put himself between Brighten and Bowie. "That seems to be, my dear Colonel, the most popular sentiment from those he meets."

Bowie pushed Franklin out of the way to address Phoenix. "Forgive me, but we must get to why we so rudely popped in unannounced. I am here to apologize for ever doubting your being the one."

This clearly agitated Phoenix. "The one what?"

Once again, Bowie was on his own train of thought, and ignored her last question and answered the first. "Neither domestic nor international, luv. The bomb my dear Franklin speaks of is of a more celestial nature." Bowie paused to take a huge hit, and drew out the moment before exhaling in Adonis's direction. "Think Roswell. And darling, you better believe there are real monsters hiding in the shadows."

Phoenix tried to clear her head and focus only on this completely exoteric statement, bizarre as it was coming from supernatural entities posed as long dead men dressed up in weird costumes. They didn't pose a threat, besides if they did, she was sure Sean Anthony would have become involved. "So if what you say is true, why in the world would they hide in the shadows playing peekaboo instead of hi, here we are; can we talk? However, that probably got old quick after a few anal probes; seen one ass, seen 'em all. So the question remains, how can Aaron use them against us if they do exist?"

"Don't exist? Are you kidding me girl?" Adonis flashed back to his early twenties when his curiosity about aliens on Earth became one of the main reasons he became a hacker. "You do know the United States government has spent the last seventy-five years hiding that there are many varieties of aliens all around the world. How do you think technology exploded so quickly after Roswell?"

Before Phoenix could argue, Adonis rambled on. "Microtechnology, stealth, Hot Pockets, and nearly everything else we shut down came from extraterrestrials."

Phoenix reached up to put her hand over her babbling companion's mouth. "Down big guy. As much as I would like to believe we didn't screw up the planet all on our own, why would a species so advanced they can bend the rules of physics to travel vast distances want to stick around to aid us? Besides, the government types can't wipe their ass without anyone who is paying attention knowing about it, so how could they keep something so big under wraps for the last seven decades?"

Franklin explained how. "Try centuries my little princess." He reached over to pinch Phoenix's cheeks, which she avoided. "In fact, Mr. Bowie and I have known about them for millennia. Normally quite peaceful with a touch of live and let live sensibilities, except for that little fascination they have for your asses. Of course, that is unless their self-interests are involved. I for one know of a time when…"

Like a little boy who found something shiny under the Christmas tree, Adonis interrupted. "I knew they were here." Then the implications of such radical news hit home. "Are you telling us aliens are living here on Earth and they are about to become a part of what is going down?"

Franklin thought for a moment, and then shrugged his shoulders. "My dear boy, we are all aliens, and it is only the hubris of your species that believes otherwise. Do you believe your consciousness materialized out of thin air?"

Bowie glanced down at the watch wrapped around his wrist. "All of this is just dandy, but I think we have overstayed our time here. You now have so much more to contemplate, and we really should be going."

By now, a very confused Phoenix needed more information. "How does any of what you shared help our current situation one bit? How are we supposed to do something about aliens we don't have a clue about, or how to find them?"

"So many questions." Franklin gave his best smile, and in another green flash, both he and Bowie vanished.

"Not cool. I don't care who the fuck they are, you don't mess with a brother's head like that. Are we the only ones who can't pop in and out whenever we feel like it? When do we get clued into that shit?"

After contemplating it, Phoenix now took something completely different from the encounter. "It isn't bigger than us. It is us."

"So now you're going to start talking in riddles too? It's time for me to crawl into a bottle right next to the most horny-ass bitch I can lay my hands on. If your big brain comes up with something for me to do, you won't know where to find me, at least until late tomorrow afternoon, and then I'll probably still be too messed up to do you any good." The whole time Adonis talked, he gathered some of his belongings and headed to the door. Before he left, he looked around at all of the glass windows. "Damn, how can anyone work in a place where everyone can see you all the time?"

"Have fun," Phoenix called out as the door closed behind him.

Colonel Brighten was at a loss. "Well that was interesting. Should I prepare to fight aliens now?"

Phoenix only shrugged her shoulders. "If aliens do attack, you should be with your people."

"Happy to have served with you, Miss Phoenix." The Colonel saluted, turned, and left with her staff, leaving Phoenix happy to be alone with her thoughts for the first time since she fully awakened in the cave in China.

<hr />

The death of the two Spanish monarchs created the first real crisis since the Enterprise had arrived in the Mediterranean. Before Sean and Alicia could settle into their seats in the CIC, she attempted to set their new priorities. "The first action we should take is to launch an E2D Hawkeye reconnaissance bird to find out the disposition of the Spanish Army around Alcazar Castle."

Sean smiled at Alicia's decision to want to focus on their part of the mission instead of contacting Captain Daily through the E2D already flying north in support of the French operations. "How about we launch the recon mission and then find out how the other half of our force is doing. I'm sure by now Captain Daily is wondering if we have forgotten about him."

Though usually the most grounded of people, the brutal nature of Aaron's visit had brought out a manic side of Alicia that Sean had never seen before. This created a laser focus on her main objective at the cost of any of the other elements in play. She had forgotten Daily was one of their priorities.

"You're right. Launch the Hawkeye north first."

Ten minutes later, the Enterprise catapulted an E2D Advanced Hawkeye off the deck headed to recon the Spanish Army. After it cleared the carrier, two F-35s, led by Captain *Dash* Nelson hooked up to the catapults and waited.

Sean would contact Captain Daily through the northern Hawkeye, while Alicia stayed in command of the one on a course to Segovia to discover how fast the Spanish Army had congregated. When the E2D reported the Spanish forces were only six hours ride from Alcazar Castle, she ordered three Seahawks with fifteen SEALs aboard to commandeer the fortress. Alicia wanted to minimize the Spaniard's casualties with the use of overwhelming force, so she ordered twenty Marines to gear up and load onto four Seahawks to support the SEALs with perimeter defense.

"I have to admit those who run this place were not especially thrilled when we pulled up to the docks, but the F-35 Lightning flyover you ordered made them more amiable to our presence." Renée had finished meeting with the town leaders and was giving Sean her report from the city as the last of the helicopters took off. "So far there isn't any news from outside of Valencia. I estimate at least fifty percent of the population decided to go visit their out of town in-laws after we showed up."

"Glad to hear. Reconnaissance has reported a large movement of troops gathering around Segovia. Once a Seahawk returns, Alicia and I will be headed there."

Renée gave Sean one final piece of advice before she signed off. "Better make sure you read all the info I put on your desk about the duality of the crown. With both monarchs dead, the houses of Castile and Aragon are sure to be pissed off, and looking for someone's head on a pike. Good luck."

Sean took one look at the pile of files on the floor next to his chair and sighed. "I know they told us when we went into the Academy that historical perspective would be a large part of our jobs, but this is ridiculous."

Alicia walked over and picked up half the pile. "Be thankful that outside of our need to keep logistics reports, we haven't had to file a single report with Norfolk."

The pilot of the E2D Hawkeye flying over the countryside of northern France picked up search radars two hundred twenty miles to the north. "Let's see if anyone is home."

With this, the radio operator began to call out the Shiloh's call sign. "Whiskey, Tango, Bravo, Yankee, this is Rough Rider. Do you copy? Over."

After five minutes of repeated attempts, they finally received a response. "This is Whiskey, Tango, Bravo, Yankee. Nice to hear your voice Rough Rider. Over."

"Is Captain Daily available to report? Over."

"Give us ten to establish contact. He is in meetings in London… Over."

Meetings was a liberal term to describe that at the moment, Daily rode in the back of the royal carriage through the streets of the city with the Queen seated next to him. Above them, the sight of a Seahawk flying cover still amazed Elizabeth.

"Here you sit as mortal as I, yet command magic that even the most imaginative sorcerer cannot conceive of. How is this possible?"

Since his audience with King Henry VII at Windsor Castle, Daily had spent the last three days exerting his control over the country's power structure. After a brief but bloody battle with the Lord of Essex and his army after his refusal to enter negotiations, the rest of the King's Lords and merchants meekly gave in to the new reality.

While they hammered out an agreement over the next three days, Daily used every chance he could to interact with the beautiful Queen. His pretext for this outing was to witness for himself how the average citizen of the city lived, but the first thing he had to adjust too was the awful smell that weighed down the air he breathed like a moldy blanket.

Looking out at the window of the elegant carriage, the contrast outside could not be starker. The drab impoverished people he saw shuffling by briefly took note of the royal carriage and the troops surrounding it as they passed. "How can you expect people to live in such squalor?"

"It is simply a fact which is beneath the notice of the King and his counselors. They fear any change in the peasant's fortunes will threaten their wealth and power."

Though there was an element of anger in her words, Daily sensed more of a weariness, as if the reality had worn her spirit down. "First thing we are going to do is We will put people to work building a sewage system that will get rid of some of the diseases that come from drinking polluted water. At the same time, we will teach your people how to create a system that can provide clean drinking water."

Her only response was a smile and her piercing, crystal blue eyes that bore right through to his soul and made his pulse quicken. Lucky for him, before she could realize how nervous she made him feel, the radio by his side came to life. He grabbed it and responded, "This is Daily, over."

"We have established contact with the enterprise through one of the Hawkeyes. Is this a good time to connect you to Admiral Phillips?"

"That's a Rodger, patch him through."

Over the next twenty minutes, Daily gave Sean a status report on his progress, and based on their overall successes, Sean decided there wasn't any reason to unite their forces for now. Best guess about when they could attempt to do so was within a month after Central Europe to the Atlantic coast would be under their political control. When they got that far they would meet in Paris. Their next contact would come in a week at the same time.

Elizabeth listened to the exchange with fascination, and when Daily finished the call, she couldn't wait to question him. "Is it possible for you to take me to see your warship?"

"Just as soon as I can find a spot for my helicopter to land." He couldn't believe how much he sounded like a teenager anticipating his first kiss. He straightened up and regained control over his hormones. "That is if you are not afraid to fly?"

The excitement in her eyes and her widening smile said this would not be a problem.

The vision of a popular British series run on PBS ran through his head. "Eat your heart out Downton Abbey."

"Downton Abbey?"

Sean and Alicia were in the air heading toward Alcazar Castle when news from the forces Alicia had sent there to subdue its defenders had gone off with only two minor casualties. Three broken ribs sustained from a broadsword to one unlucky Marine, and an arrow that had punctured a SEAL's hand.

From his vantage point 500 feet in the air, Sean could see the camps of the advance Spanish forces the Marines and SEALs had driven off earlier scattered throughout the countryside. In the late afternoon light, Sean could make out other encampments going up as additional forces arrived, while others erected earthworks.

Sean couldn't be happier with their disposition. "Looks like Renée hit a home run. They aren't going anywhere."

"It will make it a lot easier than going castle to castle in white shirts, black tie, and pants. 'Good afternoon. Is the master of the castle home? We have some exciting news to share with you about our lord and savior if you have a moment.'" Alicia laughed at the image. "Besides I left my bicycle at home."

The light nature of their banter helped to keep the terrorizing images of Aaron's sadistic traipse through the history of brutality at bay.

When their Seahawk landed, one of the SEALs stood waiting for them. Sean went straight to the issue at hand. "Where have you laid their bodies?"

"In the throne room," the SEAL Lieutenant reported. "We did the best we could to clean them up and found some of their royal clothes to dress them in. We have a few of the nobles in one of the rooms close by. I figured they would be the ones you wanted to interrogate first."

They continued to walk as Alicia talked. "Not interrogate, negotiate. We are in Catholicism central. Not only are the nobles not going to like that Isabella and Ferdinand are dead, but it also gives them a rallying cry to unite the population against us. The only way to keep this simple is to convince them we didn't kill the royals. Barring that outcome, we hit the ruling class fast and hard before they can rouse too much opposition or it could get real messy in a hurry."

Upon entering the castle, the SEAL led them half way down a long hall, and turned into a large room where six fully armed SEALs watched over a small group of self-important looking nobles. The SEAL leaned close to Sean. "The one you see rubbing his chest took two hits from stun guns before going down. My guess is he's your target."

"Thank you Lieutenant." Sean then turned to Alicia. "What do you say we give the gentlemen a show?"

Alicia agreed. "We are losing daylight. First thing though, we should let them pay their respects."

Sean turned to the SEAL. "Give the order for an hour from now, Lieutenant."

"Yes Sir." The Lieutenant saluted and withdrew.

The man the SEAL had pointed out carried an aura of superiority, even among the company of the other nobles in the room. His elaborate silk robe clothing, and the oversized cross that hung from his neck immediately identified him to a surprised Alicia. "I can't believe I am saying this, but, I didn't expect the Spanish Inquisition."

Alicia's reference at first confused Sean. "Really, Spanish Inquisition?"

Alicia couldn't take her eyes off the nobleman. "That man is the Inquisitor General of the Spanish Inquisition, Toms de Torquemada."

"How did you leap to that conclusion? I mean after all how do you know what he looked like?"

"Catholic girl, remember? The church keeps everything, including the portraits of its most sadistic members." Alicia began to struggle to keep a straight face.

A still slightly confused Sean asked, "Okay, I get it, but what do you find so funny about that?"

Alicia took a couple of deep breaths and explained. "That man in there is the real deal, and better still for us, an important cog in the Catholic Church's chokehold on 15th Century politics, yet all I can see is the song and dance number from Mel Brooks, History of the World Part I."

"Yeah, I figured that part out from your first comment."

Alicia ignored Sean's obvious sarcasm while she regained her composure. "What I'm trying to say is all we have to do to get him to cooperate is threaten him with his own chosen form of Christian cleansing circa the 15th Century, like a good old fashioned burning at the stake, or maybe the rack."

Alicia walked over to one of the SEALs and asked for his stun gun, which he handed over. She then walked straight over to the sadistic bastard with a smile on her face. The look of pure hatred in his eyes told her the viper would rip her throat out if given half a chance. She made a show of curtsying in the tradition of the court, which left the opening move to him.

He reluctantly returned the formality before the accusations began. "Are we here to be executed in the same manner as our beloved King and Queen?"

Alicia replied in perfect Spanish. "I am sorry for the loss to the families of Castile and Aragon, the church, and all of their subjects, however you are mistaken Inquisitor General, we did not murder the King or Queen. We arrived too late to save them from those who are the true unbelievers."

Torquemada turned away and addressed the other nobles. "It is the position of the Church that these are minions of the Fallen Angel Satan..." was as far as he got before Alicia zapped him with the stun gun.

Alicia turned to Sean. "If taken in the right context, these things make great party favors." She handed the spent weapon back to the SEAL. To the others in the room she now took a less measured approach. "We will not be trifled with. There will be no lies from our lips, so when I say others murdered your King and Queen, it means I will not tolerate a lack of belief. Let the houses of Castile and Aragon know that upon the morrow at midday there will be a proclamation to announce the dawn of a new day. For now, you may see to the royal funeral arrangements."

Alicia dismissed the nobles without so much as a by your leave. The humbled nobles slowly exited with a few backward glances at the still twitching Torquemada.

This was the escorting SEALs cue to march their charges to the throne room, leaving Sean and Alicia alone with Torquemada.

When they had gone, Sean almost broke down laughing. "Seriously, on the morrow? Someone has watched way too much PBS."

"Study your history on Franklin at the court of Louise XVI and his coonskin cap. All smoke and mirrors, lover boy. Shall we show our guest the proclamation now?"

Alicia posed to throw a glass of water to revive Torquemada when a SEAL burst into the room. "It looks like the charge of the light brigade is headed our way. Orders Sir?"

Get the birds in the air, and then grab the nobles who were here and take them up to the parapets." Sean grabbed his radio. "Captain Nelson, over."

"Captain Nelson reporting, over."

"It looks like the party is starting early. I need you to move up the time table to fifteen minutes from now, over."

"Can do, Sir. First pass warning, second pyrotechnics, over."

"Affirmative, over."

Alicia threw the water hard on Torquemada's face, causing him to bolt upright sputtering. Sean ordered two of the SEALs who had remained in the hall to grab him, and they headed upward.

When they reached their aerial perch, they could see two columns of cavalry galloping hard to reach the two main gates into the castle, while the three Seahawks circled above at 500 feet. Sean watched as the pilots of two of the Seahawks tilted forward and began a slow dive on the horses, blowing up enough debris with the rotors to drive the blinded horses back. When the dust in the air cleared the field, the approaches to the castle were empty, so the Seahawks moved into formation like dragons perched on the castle towers.

Sean turned his attention to Alicia. "They're all yours."

When she addressed the nobles, she had to raise her voice above the noise of the hovering craft, which added to the sense of drama. "As you can see, we have shown great restraint by not killing your fellow countrymen. If you do not agree to a parley, many wives, daughters, and sons will mourn the death of their loved ones."

With perfect timing to drive her point home, Captain *Dash* Nelson's group of eight F-35s, split into groups of two screamed below them not more than 100 feet off the deck, first from the north, then south, east, and west, each time spiraling upward immediately after in a maneuver the Blue Angeles would be proud of. The noise drowned out even the ability to think, and when Sean looked down, he saw every noble including Torquemada on the floor, shaking, with their hands over their heads.

Sean keyed his radio. "Mission accomplished, Captain, over."

"Affirmative, wish I was there to see their faces, over."

Ten minutes later, two of the captive nobles, one from the House of Castile, the other from Aragon were outside of the gates holding their family banners. Sean and Alicia watched as six horses with riders in full armor galloped toward the group. Three lords from the House of Castile and three from Aragon, all looking extremely unnerved from the flyover stopped short of their two brethren.

Alicia and Sean watched from above, amused at the excited state of the men below. "You have to admit the pageantry of it all is incredibly romantic. Makes me want to be saved." Alicia squeezed Sean's arm to drive her point home.

"You wish – like you could ever be the damsel in distress."

"I don't know, Sir Lancelot, I can think of a few things on me that could use some saving, growl."

"You are definitely beginning to worry me."

After striking a quick flick of her tongue across her lips, Alicia returned her attention to the rather animated discussion at the castle gate. Finally, the two nobles turned to walk back through the gates, followed by the six newcomers.

"Shall we greet our guests?" Sean offered Alicia his arm and escorted her back to the grand room where they first met the nobles, struck a relaxed pose in front of the massive fireplace, and waited.

The nobles entered the room with all the solemnness expected at a funeral and tried to maintain a defiant stance in the middle of the room. Sean and Alicia had decided to exclude Torquemada, and therefore the church, from negotiations they hoped would lay to rest their culpability in the death of the royals, and advance the groundwork for the Pope's proclamation.

Alicia took a step forward, and once again curtsied.

A powerful man of stature stepped forward, took her hand, and kissed it before taking two steps back and bowing. "I am Juan Diego Garcia Bartolome, Duke of Castile, and I represent the House of Castile and our grievance to those who murdered my cousin, Isabella."

"One cool customer," thought Alicia. "Not a mention about our display."

"Let me first express our sorrow at the loss of such a kind and gentle ruler, and to assure you we came here to honor the King and Queen. We have watched her impressive reformations and her genuine concern for the rights of all her subjects. We have the knowledge of those responsible for her tragic death, and we will mete out the appropriate punishment when the time comes. It is my hope that at this time we can assuage any grievance you may have against us."

The Duke cut straight to the chase. "This is yet to be proven fact; however, we will delay judgment based on your intentions."

"You're good," Alicia thought, as she decided to keep countering this byzantine protocol would take days, so she dropped the pretext. "Here is the lay of the land Duke. Isabella and Ferdinand made a point of transferring power from the nobility to town councils and the like, so forget about returning to the fractured state your country was in before their rule. That will not change, and we are here to speed up the process. Work with us, and you and your family keep most of your lands and titles; mess with us and you will rot in your own dungeons. Am I clear?"

The air went right out of the room as Juan Diego Garcia Bartolome wrestled between the poles of drawing his sword or…, he couldn't form an alternate answer.

Though they hid it well, he and his cohorts were terrified of these aliens with chariots that rocketed through the sky, fire-breathing dragons with strange rotating blades of steel, and soldiers with impenetrable clothing armed with projectiles of iron and fire. Better not to fight what they couldn't conceive of beating, so pragmatism would rule this day. Besides, the violent overthrow of an existing power structure was a practice that went back to the very beginning of humanity's experience with *civilized* society, and was as ingrained in the ruling class as servitude was in the peasants. It didn't hurt that Alicia promised the retention of the nobles lands and titles.

Once the nobles returned to their armies with news of an agreement, they quickly broke camp and dispersed back toward their own lands, while Sean and Alicia had one more task to perform. "Shall we head to the dungeon?"

Sean motioned Alicia to lead the way. "You think he will be a little more malleable this time?"

Alicia looked forward to the challenge. "Not really, but it should be fun getting to know one of history's most notorious sadists."

When they entered the dark and dank dungeon, they could barely make out the stripped naked man hanging from shackles attached to the wall. For effect, in the corner stood the same caldron with the same glowing red-hot poker Aaron used to torture them.

Sean walked over and winced before he picked the poker out of the fire while Alicia walked over and stood next to Torquemada. With an exaggerated southern drawl, Alicia asked the Pope's messenger of death, "Did you miss us?"

The next day, with sweat pouring out of every one of his pores, Torquemada delivered the Pope's proclamation. As he read, teams of newly imported sailors, accompanied by Marines for security, swarmed the countryside to impart some basic medical knowledge and care that immediately improved the lives of the local impoverished Spanish population. They began to grow in numbers around their makeshift clinics as word traveled about the many medical miracles they performed.

Alicia did her best to help by gathering the limited amount of available female sailors to bring relief to the many poor, malnourished suffering women in threadbare clothing that were everywhere she looked. The female sailors did their own form of triage by handing out food and extra clothing requisitioned from the more affluent. The image of their gaunt bodies now wrapped in the finest fashions of the day reminded Alicia of the rail thin patrons who frequented the cocaine-fueled nightclubs of the 1980s.

For now, the politics were much easier to deal with, as the few nobles who persisted in trying to ferment rebellion were completely unaware of the listening devices planted in their supposedly secure lairs.

Once again, contrary to his carefully laid plans, Aaron found himself on the losing end. "How did Sean Anthony find out so quickly I had gone to the world of 1492?" Aaron's frustration that every time he made a move against Sean Anthony's interests, the counter was already in play to thwart his devious machinations. "I destroy San Francisco, and an entire naval task force disappears without a trace. We successfully eliminated almost everyone who could oppose our plans to declare martial law, and within two weeks, I lose the support of both of my corporate and religious supporters. I spend a human lifetime rising to become the most influential powerbroker in the world, and he throws together a few malcontents, who in short order manage to not only crash the world's digital order, but end several regional wars all at once."

Aaron knew from the beginning that he would not receive any overt support from his mother Durius, who lusted after the brutal destruction of his father's parasitic creatures more than he did, but this was ridiculous. Worst still, the number of units loyal to his coup attempt had shrunk down to the point where he only controlled rural tracks in the southern states. His deal with the Devil was the only option he had left.

"Let' see if Sean Anthony and his pets have a counter to the mayhem my little Grey friends are about to unleash."

In the Canadian Rockies, buried so deep in a cavern no human could access it, stood a scene right out of a science fiction movie. Throughout the massive cave, alien structures dominated the interior landscape. Anyone familiar with the stone blocks that littered the high-altitude plateau near Tiwanaku, Bolivia in the Andean mountains known as Puma Punku would have recognized the architecture.

In the center of the complex sat a massive platform where dozens of cigar-shaped craft rested, while furtive shapes scurried in and out delivering supplies. To the casual observer, it looked as if preparations were underway to vacate the complex.

Minutes later the first of the cigar-shaped craft lifted off the cave floor and began to make its way toward the ceiling of solid rock. Just when it seemed the alien craft would crash into it, the rock dissolved to reveal an opening over a football field in diameter. In rapid succession, the rest of the vehicles silently rose into the night sky, sensed only by the bats that scattered at the disruption. Once free of the cavern, they disbursed to all points of the compass and raced to their targets, the major urban centers of the world. All around the world, UFO reports swamped civil and military radars as hundreds more exited from their own hidden locations.

It only took minutes for the alien space ships to arrive simultaneously 50,000 feet over their individual targets. Thirty seconds later, a strange apparatus deployed underneath each one and emitted an advanced electromagnetic generated field that created a massive rapidly expanding blast wave. The effect was catastrophic, as the blast wave disrupted the electromagnetic forces that bond all material together. The homes people inhabited, the cars parked in their driveways, the skyscrapers that dominated the urban centers, and ultimately every living organism on the planet began to simply fall apart.

Adonis had just arrived from his night of carousing when they felt the first rumblings of the approaching disaster. Being in California right on top of the San Andres fault, his first thought was earthquake. He was about to push Phoenix under the closest desk, when he checked the view from the penthouse of the Carlson to see something strange happening to the surrounding buildings. "Holy shit! Everything is melting!"

When the walls of the room around them began to do the same, it was time to panic. However, when Adonis looked at Phoenix, all he saw was a calm smile on her face as she calmly took his hand and informed him, "Time to go."

"Go where?" Adonis frantically asked, while the green mist swirled around them as the walls of their suite disappeared.

From Europe to Asia, India, Australia, and the continents of the Western Hemisphere, everything melted. From the elitist members of the Fortune 500 right down to the simplest single-celled microbes, nothing survived intact.

As the individual storms of deconstructed matter came together into one apocalyptic mass that encircled the globe, the electromagnetic generators on the spaceships shut down, and the Greys immediately warped away from the planet. When the worldwide Armageddon reached its greatest fury, it unleashed the most explosive energy discharge Earth had experienced since the Great Permian Extinction, which was the last time the Greys deployed the technology to wipe the slate clean at Durius's behest.

In the center of the maelstrom and immune to the chaos swirling around them, Aaron witnessed the cataclysm with his mother now by his side. "I would have preferred that you managed it by yourself." Durius turned to face her son, to see his wicked smile, as he envisioned the terror of billions of people as they melted into oblivion. Without any warning, she violently slapped it right off his face. "Years of preparation and planning so you could be the one who avenges his mother's slight, and you left it for others to clean up the mess you made of it?"

Aaron tensed, as if ready to strike back, but practical thinking prevailed, that and he knew she could crush him like a bug if he did. Instead, his smile returned. "You wanted them gone – now they're gone. Who cares as long as my dear brother suffers?"

Durius clenched her fists in rage. "You knew not to involve any other outside faction, moron, and without consulting me, you decided to act on your own. Now you have given those idiot Greys something to lord over me, not to mention the others who will now become involved."

"The Greys provided more help than you were willing to offer me, *mother*. Maybe if you hadn't been off playing while I did all the work, we might have achieved your glorious victory."

As the storm began to subside, Durius and Aaron were so busy casting recriminations at each other they failed to notice a barely perceptible sliver of continuity on the east coast of what used to be the United States.

The End of Part I

Part II
Taking Control

Taíno Symbol for Contented Sun God

Admiral Sean Phillips and his Chief of Staff Admiral Alicia Calhoun sat with Captain Mark Daily at a conference table in the Palace of Westminster in February 1494.

"I hope he doesn't expect us to bow down in his presence."

"I don't know. He has always struck me as regal in bearing."

"Doesn't having a wife back home kind of complicate matters a bit? I mean the Protestant Church isn't supposed to come in existence under Henry VIII until after the Pope denied his divorce to Queen Catherine?"

"Are you two done yet?" Captain Daily knew he would take a fair amount of abuse about his romance with Queen Elizabeth, but Sean and Alicia hadn't let up on him since their arrival four hours earlier.

After a year of shuttling orders back and forth from the continent to Daily in England, Sean felt the political situation had stabilized well enough to sail the Enterprise out of the Mediterranean. The Big E, cargo ship Cesar Chavez, fleet oiler Patuxent, and the attack submarine Indiana had entered the English Channel and arrived at the mouth of the River Thames. With Tony holding down the fort in France, Renée handling the court in Spain, and Captain Turner in Rome, the continent's populations quickly saw their lot in life improve a hundred fold.

Sean, working with Alicia and the Admiral's Staff, had interspersed over 3,000 task force personnel in groups of 25 consisting of: 6 Marines for security, 7 support staff, 6 medical personnel, and 6 educators in how representative government worked. They also set up schools to educate the illiterate populace. Each group rotated out every three months so they could experience both time on land, and receive their own lessons on 15th Century European culture back at their ships.

Alicia laughed at Captain Daily's discomfort. "I don't know, Mark, I still believe there are many more nuggets to be gleaned at your expense. I mean, how could you of all stoics get yourself in the middle of such a soap opera?"

Sean jumped in before Daily could defend himself. "It certainly complicated matters when we had to explain to the royal houses of Europe how their distant relative left the King of England for a mere Captain associated with the likes of us."

"It isn't as if I planned any of it, though having to explain myself to you two, who took over twenty years to figure it out is a bit of a stretch."

"Touché." Alicia decided enough was enough. "All joking aside, you seem to be making it work."

"Once I explained to Henry that his throne was secure and that I would supply him with a bodyguard of five Marines he settled down and accepted his loss. To tell you the truth it didn't hurt that the hidden cameras in the royal bedchamber picked up who he shared his royal vitality with. The pervert even wanted us to give him the means to record his own copies when we showed them to him."

The three sat around a table in the original Westminster Hall, which sat on the shore of the River Thames and had been the center of the British government since the 11th Century.

"How about we get down to business? As you know, I want to take the Enterprise back to Cuba, and there were numerous arguments in Paris about who should stay, who should go, and who would have control over what part of the continent. I have to say, Mark, it is nice to sit down with someone who is happy to stay right where he is."

"And Tony?"

Alicia gave Mark her *duh* look. "Of course. Initially Sean wanted him back in the Americas because he has a history there, but with Renée's talents indispensable here, there wasn't any way to get him to budge. We even had to keep them in adjoining countries."

"It isn't as if you two were going to let three thousand miles of ocean separate you either."

"It's funny how Tony finally figured out how to use the same argument against us as well." Sean shuddered when he thought back to the look on Tony's face when he first proposed that he return to Cuba without Renée.

"So that leaves Tony in overall command, with me as his second?" Daily asked.

"Correct," Sean answered. "Tony is in charge in Paris and with all matters of personnel, but the diplomatic end will be best kept with you, Renée, Tony, and Captain Turner convening in Paris every three months with representatives from all the concerned countries, including for now the Pope. The remaining ships in the Mediterranean will stay put for now. Their orders are to change ports to project power once every three months in order to keep anyone who thinks they can challenge us guessing. This action will also have the added bonus of keeping their hulls clear. We figured we could stretch out their fuel supplies before they are incapable of returning to the Americas. Hopefully we will be able to refine enough from the natural the oil seeps that it won't matter."

Then in a nod to brutal honesty, Sean added, "It could be many years before we see each other again."

Knowing he could spend the next few years without the worry of separation from his new love caused Daily to relax. "So what protocols have you set in place if everything in the Americas or here goes to Hell?"

"I can tell you the only way that could happen is if you all suddenly decide to start killing everyone in sight while declaring yourself the reincarnation of Ra, the Egyptian Sun God. By the way Mark, nice job landing that fine piece of tail. Personally speaking, I always preferred them while still a princess."

With the look of shock that was on Daily's face, Sean and Alicia didn't need to turn around to see who was attached to the voice. "I figured that after a year without your presence we were done with you," Sean added with a snarl.

Bowie smiled as he slowly walked around the table to face him. "Just because I took a well-deserved vacation didn't mean I had forgotten about my fish out of water friends. Besides I thought it would a good time to congratulate you for not screwing things up too badly since you arrived here. Also Franklin wanted me to send Tony his regards."

"As you can see Tony isn't here, but we can direct you to his location if you like?" Alicia made sure to accent her words with the proper amount of disdain. Her sarcasm faded when she could see that this time Bowie looked old and brittle. "What happened to you?"

"If one is to truly emulate the character one is playing, one must see it all the way to the end," Bowie responded in a simulated creaky voice.

"Is that why you appear to be wrapped in rags that smell like they came out of a coffin?" Then quickly shaking his head, Sean asked Bowie, "Never mind, why are you here?"

Sean preferred to end this impromptu meeting as quickly as possible.

Alicia on the other hand couldn't take her eyes off of him. She remembered the shock of the real Bowie's sudden death on the morning of January 10, 2016, only two days after the release of his last album, Blackstar. The current condition of the supernatural being's manifestation of David Bowie eerily mirrored the video for his song Lazarus. "I know I'm going to regret saying this, but for some unfathomable reason I've occasionally missed your presence over the last year."

No sooner had she finished than Bowie went through a miraculous change that transformed his sickly appearance to that of his alter ego, Ziggy. He sat on the table in front of her, leaned back on one arm, and gave her his most seductive pose. "Does that mean there is still a chance we might be able to ditch that drip of a husband of yours so you can experience a true master at work."

Her look of menace only made him worse. "Throwing darts in lovers eyes – ouch. I know luv, you would like him to stay and watch."

Sean had to laugh at Alicia's expense. "You did say you would regret it." Sean rose from the table, and walked over to the window that overlooked the River Thames. "So once again, why are you here?"

Bowie gave Alicia a wink, and rolled off the table. "Well if you are going to take all the fun out of it, I might as well get on with it."

The next second found Sean and Alicia in a completely different palace. Seated at a grand table was Tony, Renée, with Franklin standing behind them, as if expecting their arrival.

Franklin greeted them with a slight bow. "So glad to see you again."

"So didn't we leave here yesterday?" Alicia walked over and gave Tony a hug. "Which begs the question, why not then for your theatrics?"

"Franklin wanted some alone time, and he didn't want to interrupt your business."

Still wearing his Ziggy persona, Bowie strutted around the room like a feral cat, which to Alicia's eyes made him look like he would have fit right into a production of the play Cats.

Franklin decided it was best to get to the point. "We felt it would be nice to let you know that the powers that be couldn't be more pleased at all you have accomplished in such short order. Out of the 9900 sailors and civilian personnel under your command here in Europe, there have only been thirteen homicides, 32 rapes, 14 attempts to profit off the misery of those you are here to help, 96 pregnancies that turned into 86 shotgun marriages, and oh yes, we can't forget your Captain Daily's little dip into the 15th Century gene pool. You think he is planning on kids?"

Alicia interrupted Bowie. "So, are you here to give us information we are already well familiar with? And since when have you ever thought to compliment our actions?"

"Don't worry luv, he's just setting the table."

Franklin shot Bowie a nasty look before he addressed the group. "Well it was only after you made the decision for Tony to stay in Europe that I thought some information of interest to all of you might be shared."

Tony could see Franklin still wasn't sure if he should share or not. "So what, are we now off to meet with George Washington at Valley Forge, or Wellington at Waterloo? You need us to keep Janis Joplin from overdosing?"

Bowie's high-pitched laughter stopped Tony short. "You must admit, old friend, that he has the measure of us." Bowie raised his finger. "Just a second." As he sat down at the table, six fat lines of white powder complete with a gold tube appeared next to three shots of Scotch. He picked up the tube, took a deep breath before he inhaled all the lines in rapid succession. A lit cigarette materialized between his fingers immediately after shooting down all the amber liquid.

"To tell you the truth, I am paying off on a bet I made with

Franklin before you began your European pacification adventure, which unfortunately I lost. He was right and I was wrong, so let me be the first person who matters to congratulate your miraculous achievement; that, and I will be sticking around to help out once you're gone."

There it was. Sean walked over and stood above Bowie. "And what is that supposed to mean? Help with what?"

Bowie looked up, a rim of white powder caked around his nostrils. "Franklin will explain that to you."

Franklin shrugged as he thought, "There isn't much they can do with the information anyway."

"Based on how well all of you and the thousands under your command have acquitted yourselves, you can look forward to another one hundred years to make sure your changes take."

The room remained quiet for a moment as the four looked at each while contemplating what Franklin meant. Renée was first to break the silence. "I don't see how a bunch of crippled, and most likely addled centurions, would be much use in any realistic sense."

"Tell them the best part," Bowie quickly added.

Franklin pulled out his handkerchief and wiped the coke from around Bowie's nose. "You may or may not have noticed how sickness or any signs of aging have not been a part of your lives since you arrived in this reality."

"We noticed." Tony thought back to the many conversations about how with all the diseases swirling around them they contracted none of them. Numerous blood tests taken by the ships doctors, had found nothing to explain why, and they all agreed there wasn't any point in bringing it up again.

"You told us in Cuba that we wouldn't age if we went to Europe," Sean added.

"Must be something in the air you breathe," Bowie mused.

Alicia had figured it out. "I think what Franklin is trying to tell us is as long as we remain in this reality we will never age and we will never be sick."

Franklin was quick with a disclaimer. "Well, at least for the next one hundred years anyway."

Sean remained quiet, until he finished the math in his head. "I can see a big problem with that."

"I don't know. An extra one hundred years in a world that has a chance doesn't sound like a bad deal to me," Tony replied, as he thought, "And I get to enjoy another century with Renée!"

"As much as I can appreciate that you have found your paradise, Tony, I think it wise to roll this little nugget around your brain. Let's for argument sake estimate that only seventy percent of the well over 10,000 sailors and civilians here and in Cuba paired off and got busy. Say 8,000 babies grew up and did likewise, now times that by four generations, with each growing old and dying in front of our forever-young selves. Sounds more like a nightmare to me."

Tony had his own idea of paradise. "Why do you assume that they wouldn't share the same longevity and wellbeing as their parents?"

Sean looked directly at Franklin as he answered Tony. "Because the main reason we are here is to be tested, and what better way to accomplish that than to present a complex idea as simple to see if we bite."

His eyes still held by Sean's, Franklin showed his devious smile as he titled his head down to see above his glasses. "I see you have figured out that there are greater things in store for all of you, but where would the adventure be if we feed you everything from a silver spoon? In regards to the disposition of any offspring, it is exactly as you surmise."

"Good old cause and effect, which is why it is my number one goal to never consider the parenting concept and let it screw up a perfectly good time," Bowie quipped. "Welcome to my world girls and boys, that is if you understand it would be absolutely impossible to stop the human imperative on a dime." A crying baby appeared in Bowie's arms, and quickly disappeared after he displayed an exaggerated expression of terror at the thought.

"This is beginning to sound like one of my humanity classes back in college." Alicia stopped the conversation short. "Who cares what or what doesn't happen one hundred years from now. Yes, we are well aware that every decision we make either validates our beliefs, or verifies that we are all full of crap. Same old shit, different day."

Embarrassed, Sean, Tony, and Renée spent a moment in silence after Alicia's brutal assessment before Tony spoke. "At least on the positive side of things, we can assume everything will still be around for one hundred years. At least that's something."

"Then there is the matter of your staying in Europe, Tony. At first, there wasn't any way that worked for me. There I went through all the trouble to educate you in the ways of the Taíno, and now to teach it all over again was not going to happen. Fortunately for you and your partner Renée, your Captain Gable and Commander Brizuela have proven a quick study with the help of your little friend, Yacahuey. Add in the Taíno you brought along returning to Cuba to share their impressions of the European heathens, and it seems there would be little for you to do anyway."

"Only try to unite hundreds of tribes into one society, that's all." Sean didn't have any illusions about what lay ahead.

"Then we will let you get on with it," Franklin stated, as Sean and Alicia suddenly found themselves back with Captain Daily.

"They are never big on the goodbyes are they?" Alicia then turned to the unfazed Daily. "How long were we gone this time?"

"Exactly twenty minutes. Where this time?"

"Back in Paris at the Louvre with Tony and Renée." Sean went on to explain to Daily the latest crazy.

"What's supposed to happen after one hundred years?"

Alicia rolled her eyes in frustration. "Here we go again."

Two days later, the Enterprise, Cesar Chavez, Laramie, and

Indiana left the English Channel behind, and began the two-week journey back to Guantanamo Bay, Cuba.

The voyage back across the Atlantic gave Sean and Alicia way too much time to speculate. "Seriously, where do you think this will all end?"

"To tell you the truth lover boy, I can't see us ever leaving here, unless Carl and Sean Anthony can stop that maniac Aaron from pulling the plug. I think we are the fallback position so that if everything else goes up in flames this would be the last sanctuary for humanity. Nothing else makes sense."

Sean wasn't convinced. "If we are the sanctuary, where did Rebecca disappear to? It seems to me if you are correct, this would be the safest place for Carl to stash her."

Alicia shook her head no. "You forget about how important she was to the 1942 reality. I bet you anything that is exactly where she is right now with her husband Carl, doing exactly what we are doing here.

"I sure wish it wasn't always at the expense of having so much distance between us and Tony and Renée," Alicia continued. "On the other hand, it might be a step forward without us always around to fix his foot-in-mouth disease."

Sean wasn't sympathetic. "Think of all the sailors and civilians with us who are away from loved ones they may never see again, and we had to leave Tony and Renée behind for a while? At least they are in the same reality."

"Amen to that."

When Sean and Alicia arrived in Guantanamo Bay, they found the crew they left behind had built a rather respectable village. There were workshops equipped with machinery removed from the cargo ship Emelia Earhart and the battleship Missouri, and generators unloaded from the ships supplied electricity to drill the wells for drinking water. The crews had also carved out of the jungle landing pads, built hangars for the helicopters, and a landing strip in anticipation of the C-2A Greyhound fixed wing aircraft returning.

With the help of Yacahuey along with Marines and Navy medical personnel, Commander Maria Brizuela had the Taíno ambassadors spread the word about the dangers from across the ocean throughout Cuba and the Caribbean. She told hilarious stories to Alicia, including one where they had to convince the terrified Taíno to board a Seahawk and fly to one of the neighboring islands.

Intermingling between the sailors and the indigenous population was inevitable, so Sean had taken the precaution before they left for Europe, of testing all to ensure there would not be any epidemics. Fortunately, between the strong leadership of Captain Andy Gable and Commander Brizuela, and the paradise qualities of the island culture, sexual assaults and every other type of violent criminal activity remained low.

Captain Andy Gable had instigated a policy that restricted the number of sailors who could associate with the Taíno at any given time. The same three-month rotation they used in Europe also lessened the culture shock to both societies and allowed for smoother integration with the easy-going nature of the Taíno. The Taíno learned to be more assertive, while their influence helped to calm down the more aggressive nature of the 21st Century sailors.

For some time after they returned, Sean left the running of the newly constructed village to Captain Gable while he and Alicia spent some alone time in the home Franklin built for Tony. However wonderful that was, both Sean and Alicia knew they had to come up with long-range plans if they were going to bring the other tribes of the Americas into their sphere of influence.

Though Captain Andy Gable had proven an able leader, three months after their return, he had his hands full dealing with the added presence of the additional sailors that had returned from Europe. Despite his best efforts, discipline was beginning break down within the ranks.

"Company is coming." Alicia had heard the helicopter approach, as she and Sean stood waiting in the small clearing. When it landed and Captain Gable stepped off, Alicia greeted him. "So what brings you to the wilderness, Andy? We were not expecting you until next week."

"As much as I would have rather waited until then, if we don't get our ships back to sea as soon as possible, we may be looking at a complete breakdown in discipline. Have you finished at least enough of a plan to resettle some of our sailors elsewhere?"

This was news to Sean. "You didn't mention any concerns the last time we visited the settlement. In fact everything appeared in order."

"When you combine the need to keep many of those who returned from Europe on their ships with the 20-to-one ratio of men to women, it didn't take much to set off a riot."

"Did this include the Taíno?" Alicia went straight to the worst-case scenario.

"Fortunately not, as it was only on the Enterprise, but I can report that the officers and MAs [Master-at-Arms responsible for law enforcement] had their hands full for a solid two days regaining control. So far, there are 120 sailors detained, and another fifty in Sickbay being treated for their injuries."

This was all Sean needed to hear. "Yes, it is possible to mount a mission to the Chesapeake Bay immediately."

Thank you, Admiral Phillips." Captain Gable saluted as Sean and Alicia headed back to the house to pack while the chopper waited.

All along Sean and Alicia had planned to settle the east coast of North America instead of the Gulf region, and they always returned to the Chesapeake as the first option. Now left without any time to spare, additional advance planning would have to be done while enroute.

Once on the helicopter, Sean's concern for the rapport they had built over the last year needed assurance. "What about the Taíno? How are they reacting?"

"Let's just say, the honeymoon will be over if we don't resettle most of our new personnel elsewhere. If at all possible, I would appreciate it if part of your plan is to keep here the same personnel that have established good relations with the locals."

"That has always been our thinking Andy. However, it would be impossible to resettle enough of our sailors around the eastern seaboard overnight to reduce the tensions. A practical timeline is what we are trying to work out. We will still have to leave many on the ships we take north, but at least that will take the pressure off the settlement." Sean knew they were on the clock, but this bad news didn't leave them with the time for a perfect solution."

"At least this will give them a sense of purpose when they see us moving forward," Alicia added.

Fifteen minutes later, they landed on the Enterprise flight deck. Captain Daniel Osaka greeted them before they all disappeared into the Admirals Ready Room. Commander Jonathan James of the attack submarine Indiana, Commander Melissa Wu of the cargo ship Cesar Chavez, Lt Commander Michelle Chen and her senior civilian officer, Bradley Franks, of the fleet oiler Patuxent, and Commander Maria Brizuela had arrived there while the Seahawk was enroute.

After the usual pleasantries, Sean gave Alicia the floor. "The plan is to establish a series of small settlements along the coast beginning at Chesapeake Bay and working back down to Florida. We start with two settlements in Chesapeake Bay, and one off of Cape Hatteras inside the Grand Banks at Roanoke Island, with enough supplies for three months and let the tribes come to them."

They all studied the nautical maps Sean and Alicia had used to plot settlement locations.

Captain Osaka was the first with a question about the sequence of locations. "I think I understand your logic, but wouldn't Long Island Sound be a better place to start than Cape Hatteras. It seems Cape Hatteras would be risky to keep supplied with its well-earned reputation as a ships graveyard."

Alicia looked up at Sean with her I told you so face, but defended the decision. "We both felt that for now the furthest we could start and still keep a close eye would be Hatteras and Chesapeake Bay. Once the settlements are established, they are both natural locations for us to expand further into the continent." She stuck her finger on the chart. "And what could be more natural than place the first one at Norfolk. Good for moral, and good to remind the sailors where they come from and what they stand for."

"Who will be in charge?" Bradley Franks worried about how all of this would affect the 200 civilians serving on the two supply ships.

"Good question, Brad," Alicia acknowledged. "The senior Marine at each settlement will command. Six of the Taíno we took to Europe and three of the crew whose ancestry goes back to the tribes who populate the area will join them. Commander Brizuela worked on this over the last month and has put together her list of the others who will fill out their commands."

Captain Gable had a suggestion. "Brad, could you survey the civilian ranks for skills like carpentry, woodworking, and anything that might help with the settlements? It turns out that the skill sets of some of the Earhart civilian crew have been tremendous assets in building our settlement."

"Will do," Brad responded thrilled to be involved.

Captain Osaka had another concern. "What about the malcontents on my ship? Are we going to leave them in detention, or get them off the ship?"

Sean had a solution. "Daniel, you will pick three groups of those who committed the worst offenses. Then, as examples to the other offenders, they will be detailed to chain gangs at each settlement until their local Marine Commander is comfortable with their rehabilitation."

Lt. Commander Michelle Chen offered up her own rather primitive solution. "Personally speaking, I think some of Brad's people could set up stocks in the town square, which would accomplish the same thing, Admiral."

As many around the conference table chuckled at the image, Sean nodded his head in mock agreement. "Trust me, Michelle, if the chain gangs don't work, a little public humiliation now and then might not be a bad thing."

"So how does this play out?" Commander Melissa Wu asked. "Land fifty sailors on a deserted shore with a shitload of food, and wait to see who is curious enough to check it out?"

"You are not far off the mark, Commander. We will land a small party of Marines with the Taíno and Commander Brizuela's selectees, set up a small camp, and wait. To begin a settlement without the locals consent would mimic too closely the assumptions of those of Columbus. With the one of our ships in plain sight at each location, it shouldn't take too long to draw the locals out. Then hopefully the Taíno ambassadors can convince them peaceful interaction is in their best interest as they have previously at several locations throughout the Caribbean."

Commander James still had questions. "Do we arm our people, and if so what happens the first time there is a misunderstanding and a local gets killed?"

Alicia waited to answer as a steward arrived and after a nod from her, served coffee. "The Marines will be armed as they are responsible for security. Besides, the Enterprise will be in the bay so Seahawks can reach the settlements in minutes for support."

Sean wanted to wrap it up. "Let's hope we are not on the way to rebuilding the original thirteen colonies, and the genocide that went along with it."

"Amen to that." Alicia added.

"Dismissed."

Two weeks later the Enterprise, the attack submarine Indiana, and the supply ships Laramie and Patuxent, lifted anchor and sailed away to the north.

Though there were numerous issues that required a delicate hand in resolving, overall the plan succeeded beyond their expectations. Within the first year, six different settlements now populated the eastern seaboard, each semiautonomous in their ability to make treaties that were mutually beneficial to the tribes and settlers. Sean and Alicia's major role in the drama was to act as The Great Chiefs. They presided over local councils that settled disagreements and decided the guilt or innocence of those accused of committing crimes. The various tribes grew to trust in the fairness of their combined judgments, so much so that Sean and Alicia resolved disputes between tribes that historically had led to warfare.

During this time, the cargo ship Cesar Chavez and the oiler Patuxent sailed to Jamaica where Bradley Franks and his civilians developed the infrastructure to supply fuel and other petroleum products from the oil and gas seeps there. Once perfected, the nuclear sub Indiana relayed this technology to Europe. With these new fuel supplies expansion could move further throughout the Americas, and surface ships could make cross Atlantic trips once a year.

Alicia's idea to disperse small numbers of Marines, sailors, and civilians in small settlements proved genius. The impact of a few people from the 21st Century integrating into the surrounding country was more successful than planting a city of thousands. This worked so well that over the following decades Sean and Alicia repeated the template all along the east coast of North America. Later, the St. Lawrence, Mississippi, and Rio Grande rivers gave them access to the western interior of North America. To the south, Commander Brizuela played the role as The Great Chief during the expansion throughout the Caribbean and along the coasts of Central and South America, including up the Amazon.

From his position on the foredeck of the John Paul Jones as it entered Guantanamo Bay, Tony fixated on the battleship Missouri sitting in a dry dock constructed for its preservation. "It's hard to believe how much history is represented in that metal," Tony said with a sigh, before he tore his eyes away to smile at his wife, Renée. "Too bad there are only a few here who understand that. Can you believe it has been over twenty years since we left for Europe?"

Renée squeezed his arm. "I'm excited to spend some time traveling around with Sean and Alicia to see what they have accomplished here."

Tony had a different take. "What you're really excited about is you no longer need to kiss all of those Royal Asses to get anything done. Thank God for Captain Daily."

Tony laughed at the thought of Daily's predicament. "Little did he know when he married Elizabeth that he would inherit most of the European Royalty as in-laws and with it all the insipid drama."

"At least he has our Navy as the final authority and Commander Thornton when things get too hot." Renée then smiled at a thought. "I would love to be a fly on the wall when he has to explain to Elizabeth why he ruled against one of her relative's interests." The sound of the ships anchor letting go interrupted Renée. "It's good to be back."

Two hours later, they sat inside a seaside cabana with Sean and Alicia. Sean stood up and lifted his glass for a toast. "Not only are we finally able to spend time with our special friends after two decades of separation, we can also take a moment to celebrate a marriage too long in the making. So may you enjoy a lifetime of joy, and may the road ahead be straight and true." They all clicked their glasses and Sean sat back down.

"Thank God you still know how to keep these things short," Tony quipped. "Let me tell you if I never have to attend another royal banquet, my life will be complete. You wouldn't believe how long-winded their presentations are when you add in the BS titles it seemed like everyone including the kitchen staff and chambermaids held."

Renée shot Tony a dirty look. "What Tony is trying to say is two decades apart was way too long. He never stopped complaining about how much it sucked that an ocean separated us from you."

Tony had his own recollections to share. "When you spend most of your time educating the population on hygiene safety, then teaching them how to engineer and build sewer systems that only flush the problem somewhere else, it can get old."

Renée shuddered when she thought back to her earliest memories. "Yeah like how the artists and philosophers of the day managed to ignore the reality of someone throwing the contents of their chamber pots out of their windows onto the streets below, and how all of that sewage worked its way into the drinking water. Thank goodness for the water filtration systems on our ships, and don't even get me started on the stench."

"Enough about who the heathens of this age really are, and instead, how about you report on the impact you had on the ground before you left." Sean wasn't under any illusions that much could change in two short decades, but he needed to know if they were on the right track.

Tony figured he would start with the bad first. "Like any other revolution through the ages, the existing power structure kisses our asses most of the time saying what we want to hear, and then spends their time alone formulating secret conspiracies. The funniest part of it all is that no matter how many times we anticipated their moves they never figured out that we listened to everything they said from the bugs we planted.

"We didn't need to make an example of any of the conspirators because the Royal Families were too busy blaming each other for being our spies and leaking their plans. It was Renée's idea to let them escalate these accusations into actual open conflict, and waiting until after a winner emerged to swoop in and the take lands and titles of all the parties involved."

Renée could see concern on both Sean and Alicia's faces, so she quickly added, "This is the best part. Without the ability to add the peasants who used to be under their thumb into their fighting ranks as cannon fodder, only those who instigated the conflicts suffered."

Tony laughed. "Some of the peasants would actually gather at the site of the battles and watch for entertainment; the medieval version of rubberneckers."

Sean wasn't amused. "So what Tony, did you hand out popcorn and candy?"

"I guess you had to be there," Tony quipped."

Alicia could see how they could spend days making fun of the many forms of ignorance of the era's rulers. "Why don't we focus instead on some of the other programs you initiated that are making the rest of the population's lives easier?"

Renée took that as her cue. "The biggest puzzle we needed to unravel entailed what form of government would work best to transition from the old to the new. Tony, Daily, and I agreed that any form of collectivism, plutocracy, oligarchy, or majority rule by the wishes of a very ignorant population would not resolve any of the problems. Therefore, we instead applied the same hierarchal form of naval rule we lived under. Surprisingly, it seemed to allow for the most freedom and reward."

Renée took a moment to take a drink before continuing. "Much to the consternation of those who still occupied Europe's thrones, except of course for King Charles VIII of France, Paris became the center of both trade and government. The main driving force was to lift the peasant's out of their poverty by bringing new products to market as quickly as possible. We started with the most basic technologies to apply, which, much to Tony's surprise, immediately gained acceptance."

Tony chimed in. "With the ability to create new products and take them to market without the fear of a military invasion every time a region acquired wealth, the need for local military protection became increasingly unnecessary."

Alicia looked out on the ships resting at anchor. "As impressive as all of this sounds, do you think we can change the course of European history with a few thousand sailors from another era handing out modern ideas like candy? What happens eighty years from now when we have run out of handouts and the powers pulling our strings make us leave?"

Renée had spent some time thinking about that same question. "Personally speaking, not a snowball's chance in Hell. You have seen as well as I have the effect two decades has had on how our people have integrated. Once our leadership by advanced technology ends and we're all dead and gone, the same old idiots will arise and take over everything we have built."

Sean struggled every day with the same doubts. "So you believe that if we remain in control for another eighty years, it won't make a difference?"

Alicia's struggle was with Sean. "What I keep trying to remind you of, is that we have an advantage no other empire possessed. We have released our technology for the public good instead of the pursuit of better ways to kill. If we succeed in creating a species that learns to live in balance within its natural resources that should mean something. At least that is how I choose to look at it, otherwise, why bother putting us here?"

"It could be that those pulling our strings wanted to add some spice to the entertainment value we provide, and figured rearranging history across realities would do the trick," Renée suggested.

Tony summed it up. "And there we are as teenagers loaded with hubris right back at the Sambo's restaurant in Hollywood revved up on ten cent coffee trying to figure out how to read everybody's mind. Let's face it folks, born to the blood philosophers we are not. I for one wouldn't have missed this part of the ride for anything, whether it was meaningful, or a complete waste of time."

Sean shook his head in agreement. "Well at least we're giving those in the Western Hemisphere a chance to be prepared this time in case the Europeans return to their bad old ways. Who knows what difference that is going to make."

"If that turns out to be the case, then we have to make sure the European's get their ass kicked when they do," Renée concluded as she smiled at the thought.

"Amen to that," Sean and Alicia answered in unison.

Over the ensuing decades, they all managed to explore most of the Western Hemisphere's vast beauty on the network of roads that now spread out to all points of the compass. However, those roads always led back home to Cuba, and the paradise it remained.

According to the dispatches from Europe provided by the *mail runs* made by the Seawolf, dispatches from all along the Americas made by the Indiana, and the dispatches from the Pacific made by the Hampton, not one of the sailors, civilians, or military personnel who arrived from the future gave a thought about the reality they left behind. Not a single member of the Enterprise Task Force had aged a year, though there were losses from traumatic injuries and the simple reality that some humans seem intent on doing stupid things. Though it appeared they all shared immortality, as promised by Franklin all those years ago, not one their offspring lived beyond previous norms. True to Alicia's concerns, this created the uncomfortable issue of not only outliving their children, but their children's, children's, children as well.

"Happy 148th birthday lover." Sean leaned down to kiss Alicia, who opened one eye when their lips touched. "I must admit you don't look a day over 120."

She grabbed a pillow and smacked it across his face. "And insulting me on my birthday is supposed to get you what?"

"Get your lazy ass out of bed and come see what I've prepared for us on the veranda." Sean threw her robe over her head before he walked out of the room. "Hurry up or all the ice will melt." It was already 90 degrees with ninety-nine percent humidity at 9:30 in the morning, which is normal for the middle of August on the tropical island.

Five minutes later she strutted sexually through the French doors, her robe wide open. "Does this look like a 120-year-old body to you?"

Before Sean could react, the female ensign who had prepared the beautiful setting on the table in front of him came into Alicia's view. She quickly covered herself with the robe and forcibly knotted the belt.

"You said you prepared it?"

Sean motioned for the red-faced ensign to retreat into the kitchen. "If I had known you were going to put on a show, I would have warned you. Come sit down."

As she crossed where he sat, she smacked him on the back of the head. "That's two strikes, you better not get a third."

"Or what?" Sean grabbed her, and sat her on his lap.

Alicia pulled her robe open to expose her breasts, and rubbed them all over his face. "Or that is the last of the girls you'll see for a while." Alicia covered back up and managed to extract herself from his hold so she could go over sit in her chair.

The view from the veranda at the home they built on a bluff overlooking the Caribbean couldn't be more beautiful as she looked out on azure seas down below.

"You would think after one hundred years of this it would get old." Alicia picked up the Champaign glass that held a mimosa and took a drink from it. "Add in that we haven't been visited or sent somewhere else by either Bowie or Franklin and I do believe we've discovered paradise."

"If you take away all of those pesky council meetings where we hear every complaint the Guilds can think up, I might agree."

Alicia wasn't very sympathetic. "Solve twenty problems, and twenty more pop up in their place. At least it is nearly impossible for the furniture guild to start a war with the electrical one. Give in or I'll run you through with my wood chisel."

Their server returned with their breakfast and placed them before them. Sean put his napkin on his lap and picked up his fork. "You mock me, but the religions some have formed still pose every bit the threat the Catholic Church used to."

Alicia sliced off a piece of ham and waved it at Sean. "And the world turns. Remember the mess we took over, and see where we are now. Native Americans assimilated into Europe, Europeans, though I admit in numbers too small to matter, in America without a single pandemic and I can say no one else could have performed better."

After a lengthy pause to enjoy their meal, Sean agreed. "Tony may not possess any of the necessary skills to navigate through political waters, but he sure hit a home run when he suggested replacing the hierarchal form of naval rule he and Renée had instituted earlier in Europe with the trade guilds of old as a form of government by council."

Alicia agreed. "It's much easier to ferret out corruption when each guild's books are a matter of public record." With a quick chuckle she added, "That guy from the guild running the ports certainly harkened back to the Mafia of old when he tried to strong arm the merchants."

Sean laughed at the memory of the man's folly. "Isn't he still swabbing the stalls on that animal freighter on the Atlantic run?"

"Beats having to build more jails," Alicia countered. "At last count, 85 percent of all criminal acts were adjudicated with judgments where the punishment fit the crime, though the old bugaboos capital punishment and abortion still plague us."

Sean shook his head in agreement. "As long as men remain out of the decision-making process on abortion, I'm fine with the women's majority either way."

With major support from Sean, Alicia was instrumental in creating new laws that removed men from all female oriented issues. However, they parted ways on capital punishment, where Sean felt strongly in a life for a life, especially when the level of violence was gratuitous. Like castration upon conviction of violent rape, both laws had to establish absolute guilt before they carried out the sentences. For those cases where the jury was unsure of the level of guilt, they built a penal colony on one of the islands of the Outer Bank to incarcerate these individuals.

Sean changed the subject. "Anyway, enough of politics and policy. We are supposed to be enjoying your birthday today. What is your wish? A lazy day curled up in bed watching a movie, a day on the water, or in town with Tony and Renée?"

Before Alicia could give voice to her choice, she heard a familiar voice coming up from behind.

"So what kind of trouble are you two planning for us now?" The next surprise Sean failed to inform Alicia of walked into view.

Alicia got up and hugged first Tony, then Renée. "That's strike three."

Sean pointed Alicia's attention to the table. "So it's my fault you didn't notice the two extra place settings?"

Tony turned to Renée and shrugged.

Sean then turned to face his friend and feigned disgust. "So do you spend most of your day trying on the most ridiculous clothing known to man, or is this how you roll out of bed every morning? Really Renée, how do you let him leave the house looking like a color-blind peacock?"

"Someone needs to counter your button-down sensibilities. Besides, after so long with the same skin he would go nuts. There are only so many ways you can rearrange hair." Renée, contrary to Tony's bold look, chose instead functionality in the tropical heat with a fuchsia colored cotton blouse, shorts, and a pair of flip-flops.

Alicia had to admit that after all the years, Tony and Renée hadn't changed much, still very much in love and the perfect complement for each other. "So did you get the territorial disputes between the Kiowa Apache and Comanche nations resolved, or are they still trying to relive the good old days?"

Tony and Renée as Special Ambassadors to the Western Hemisphere resolved political disputes under the astute direction of Brizuela and Clark. Sean and Alicia kept watch over Europe under Captain Mark Daily and the Pacific under Captain Daniel Osaka who had developed into quite the diplomat.

Daniel's former command, the USS Enterprise, stood at anchor in Guantanamo Bay unattended. With so many of her complement spread across Europe, the Pacific, and the Western Hemisphere, there were not enough sailors available to crew the Big E.

"Four generations after the need to ensure their food supplies had come to an end, and they still sneak around trying to steal each other's horses. I swear, why did we bring the horses over again?" Tony asked.

"If it wasn't the horses, they would still fight over territory or kidnapping each other's fair maidens. Old habits are hard to break," Renée argued.

"Seriously though," Alicia interjected. "We all have to admit it is pretty amazing that the tribes of the Western Hemisphere have adjusted quickly to so many changes. Here we are in the late 16th Century manufacturing private planes, electric cars, and forced air heating and cooling, with a world population stabilized at 400 million and not one attempt to blow it all up." She knocked on the wooden table for good luck.

Tony watched with pride as his mate held forth. "Enough generational changes in the population have taken place that there are only a few cultural tribalism influences left. The indigenous people from the Yaghan at the southern tip of South America to the Inuit in the northern extremes of North America mostly consider themselves as one people."

Sean shook his head in agreement. "Our representatives, some of whom are Taíno, to the Aboriginal people of Australia, the Maori of New Zealand, and the many tribes across the Polynesian islands, including the Hawaiians, have reported similar success over the years, and now they all trade with the people of the Western Hemisphere."

"Outside of Africa, China, and South East Asia where their warlords won't let go, and the Russian proclivity for oligarchs, I think we have done a good job."

Tony laughed. "Considering that our sailors stationed here had a hand in the procreation of over thirty percent of the Cuban population to date, I would say that has been well established."

"Worst of all to me is the expectation that you have to spend the time to hear about how successful someone's great grandchildren who are pushing 60 years old have become." Renée stated with a smile and a wink before she checked the watch on her wrist. "If it's all the same to everyone, I'm starving and this food isn't getting any fresher."

They all agreed, and conversation for the next hour consisted mostly of catching up on how their different friends and colleagues were doing at their various postings around the world.

After brunch ended, the four walked over to an open-top vehicle that looked like a scaled down Austin Martin. Tony unplugged it, and both he and Renée got in. "According to the gospel of Franklin, we only have another year until something happens."

"Let's enjoy the peace and quiet for as long as it lasts. Besides, only the four of us know about the 100-year mark," Sean stated as he and Alicia waved goodbye.

"Rodger that boss." With a final wave, Tony hit the pedal and drove off. A half hour later they were back at the home Franklin installed him in all those decades ago. He kept it, not because of Franklin, but because this is where Renée had returned to him from the dead. He parked the car and they headed to the door. Upon entering, they experienced their first shock in years. In the living room, Franklin and Bowie stood smiling. Seated on the couch, Sean and Alicia looked very unhappy.

"Did you miss us?' Bowie was back in Ziggy mode, while Franklin maintained his customary buttoned up brown colonial suit.

"This can't be good. What now, is there a Zargon space fleet entering Earth orbit and you need us to tickle their feet into defeat." Tony walked right by them and reached for the bottle of rum from his still.

"Zargon fleet, tickle, that is funny. I have so missed your rapier wit, Anthony." A bottle of wine appeared next to the rum. "You know I prefer wine. Would you mind pouring?"

"Since when don't you conjure up your own glass, and where's your coke and weed? Isn't that a part of your Ziggy persona?"

Bowie ignored Tony's sarcasm. "I am dressed to honor my first appearance with this lovely couple." He turned his gaze toward Sean and Alicia. "That and to compliment the four of you again for achieving such grand results. Would you mind pouring me one while you are at it, but could you make mine rum?"

Reluctantly Tony complied, and after everyone had a drink, he and Renée sat down next to each other and waited to hear how their lives were going to change again.

"You leave us here for a century..." Sean stopped short. He had a lot of time to think about this moment, and he wanted to get it right. "That's right; believe it or not we have been here for one hundred years, and after all that time, you still haven't given us a clue as to why. Is that why you are here now, to finally expose your dirty little secrets?" Sean wasn't much for delaying the inevitable.

"What no foreplay?"

Franklin motioned for Bowie to stop and then continued, totally ignoring Sean's question. "To put it simply, you are finished, and it is time to go home."

Thinking of his time with Renée, Tony frantically asked, "Wait, what about the year we have left?"

Franklin's news caused Alicia to ignore both Tony and Sean's questions. "What do you mean go home? If you refer to the place we spent less than a third of our lives, I don't believe you will get any of us to call that home now."

Then Renée voiced a concern unique to her. "My understanding was if Tony left, I would cease to exist. Is this still true?"

Franklin tilted his head down, so his eyes were above his bifocals. "My dear, by my count there are hundreds of your offspring roaming throughout the Americas. You are everywhere, and besides, I said you couldn't go, not that you would not exist."

Tony stood up so quick his drink spilled. "What the hell does that mean? If you think I am going anywhere without her, you're crazy."

Franklin dispensed with the posturing and revealed a look of genuine sadness. "For reasons that may or may not become clear to you very soon, I can only say I regret that this must be."

Franklin then leaned in close so only Tony and Renée could hear what he said. "Somewhere in the back of both of your minds, you knew this day would come. Well that day is today if there is to be any chance for the world you all so brilliantly reformed to survive, Tony must now leave it."

Sean could tell that whatever Franklin was saying that Tony was about to explode. "You know, for most of our time here, Tony has conjectured that our being here has absolutely no other purpose than to entertain some higher civilization. I think I am starting to come around to such an insane idea. What about you, Alicia, do you think they are capable of yanking our chains like that?"

Alicia had her concerns. "So what is going to become of this world if we are not here to continue to safeguard it from reverting to its old habits? Then there is that tiny little problem of after a century here all those families in this reality torn apart and our sailors returning to loved ones who haven't had time to miss them. Sounds like chaos on a monumental scale to me."

"That's up to Renée." Once again, Franklin failed to address their concerns. As the room filled with green mist, they all knew that was the way it would remain.

The last shared memory Sean, Alicia, Tony, and Renée had together was of Tony and Renée's frenzied attempt to embrace each other.

In Guantanamo Bay and everywhere else the Enterprise Task Force ships, aircraft, equipment, and personnel existed, the green mist made them all disappear. All that remained was a shocked Renée. "Son of a bitch!"

Renée collapsed on the bed crying, all alone in the house Franklin had built for Tony in Cuba. That is until a cheery voice called to her from the kitchen. "Do you prefer Scotch or Jack Daniels?"

Recognizing Franklin's voice, she called back, "Scotch," as she pulled herself together and headed for the kitchen.

"Where did you send my friends and my husband, and why am I the only one still here?" Renée gruffly demanded, knowing she would not like the answer.

Franklin put one hand on her shoulder while he handed her the tumbler of Scotch with the other. "Well child, we need someone here to make sure this planet survives in this reality, and I am sorry to inform you that you were the only viable option.

"Besides you will discover all the wonderful benefits that come with becoming a goddess; that is if you are anything like me." Bowie's clothes changed to a white flowing robe topped off with a gold laurel wreath on his head. In his left hand, he held a cardboard lightning bolt, which he now threw at Franklin.

Unknown to her, Franklin had planted the image of Renée as Mother Earth, the progenitor of all life into the consciousness of every living human being.

Renée glared back at the two before knocking down her drink in one swift motion and slamming the empty glass on the table. She wiped her mouth off, and walked over to the bar and grabbed a larger glass to pour another stiff drink. "So let me get something straight. Are the rest of my people still here, or did you ship them out as well?"

"No and yes," Bowie quipped, before Franklin answered in a kinder gentler way.

"You are the only member of the original arrivals who remains here in this reality. But before you get too upset, it does come with some valuable perks."

"Is one of them the ability to strangle the both of you?"

"Honey, if that were possible, what use would we be to you in your time of need?" Bowie answered with flair.

"Somehow knowing you two are the ones responsible, I don't take much faith in that," Renée stated. "What possible impact could I have on an entire world by myself?"

Franklin decided it best to show off. "Well, think about being anywhere in the world right now."

Before Renée could argue, she found herself, along with Bowie and Franklin, standing in her and Tony's former residence in Paris, much to the surprise of its current resident, who immediately recognized her and saluted. "Captain Aslan. How did you do that, and who are they?" Before he could get an answer, the three disappeared as quickly as they came.

Back home she grabbed the poured drink and downed it. "Was

that you or me?"

Bowie was only too happy to confirm. "That was all on you luv. Believe me when I tell you that isn't all you are capable of. Since you are the one who has to hold the world together for a while, all of your new gifts will come in handy."

Renée thought of somewhere else she would rather be, but nothing happened. Franklin looked at her and shook his head. "Your newfound powers cannot be used outside of this reality, so no, you can't follow Tony."

"Shit. So how long is this supposed to continue this way?" Renée fumed.

Franklin was downright cheerful, as he explained, "Oh not very long at all. In fact you will barely notice the time pass."

It took Franklin a couple of weeks, mostly without the irritation of Bowie's presence, to convince Renée it was in her best interest to assume the role. He also explained how she could address the responsibilities left vacant in the power vacuum created when everybody and everything with the Enterprise Task Force disappeared.

High up in the Rocky Mountains in the year 2018, one hundred fifty miles northwest of where Denver should be, a woman saddled her horse for an early morning ride. Her nearest neighbor lived twenty miles to the south, but this wasn't out of the norm for the high country, or for that matter over ninety percent of the Earth's continents. The human population on the planet held steady at around nine hundred million inhabitants.

Renée slung her leg over the horse and headed toward the path they would take for the day's ride. As the horse slowly walked through a stand of trees, she thought back to over one hundred years ago when she made the decision to step aside and let one of her many descendants administer the world's political needs.

Though she was now 538 years old, none of the children born to her carried the gene of long life, the oldest dying at the age of 92. Though she had many mates during the last three hundred years, no one ever came close to the love she still held for Captain Anthony Knox. Besides, after all of this time, she still held out hope he would return to her, after all she had carried out her end of the deal.

As Renée cantered along the trail, she thought back to the early planning meetings that laid the groundwork for humanity's future under their guidance before her husband and the rest disappeared. She remembered clearly, how the guiding principal whether an idea advanced or not was what impact it had on the planet's ecological health.

With the hindsight of five hundred years to work with, the more these ideas took root across the world, the true insanity of how humanity trashed her former reality hit home. With the one hundred years of work that had set the stage and the advantage of her elevated status, the world's people grew to look forward to the next revolutionary edict from on high. Though Renée was loath to be a part of it, Bowie always handled the buildup to the announcements, and the world would rock for a solid month before and after.

The one item Franklin insisted they put all of their efforts into once industry caught up was the one that baffled her most. The system entailed evolving the electromagnetic generated fields generated by Specter, amplifying the strength of its signal a hundred fold, and fitting it all into a series of satellites launched into geosynchronous orbit.

True to Franklin's unwillingness to share why, he never gave her any details about the nature of the threat. Renée knew from years of experience that it would be a waste of time to ask. The satellites and their ground tracking stations that made up the system became operational toward the end of the 20th Century.

"Without a threat to worry about, why build a defense system that is more complex than anything developed in my old world?" Renée uttered these words to her horse as she looked about the unsullied beautiful paradise that surrounded her.

"Enough of this damn introspection!" She gave her horse a hard kick to the flanks, which sent the mare off in a full gallop, straight into a sudden wall of green mist. When the startled horse burst through to the other side, she was riderless.

The fleet of triangular craft suddenly appeared high above the world Renée had just exited, and were immediately horrified to find they had a welcoming committee in the form of concentrated shocks to their spacecrafts. The trap Renée spent decades creating without knowing why closed. Within seconds of their arrival in the skies above, each ship shook violently until the stress blew them apart. The multitude of explosions generated so many pieces they resembled mini nebulas. Franklin stood on the patio of the home he had replicated to match Tony's Cuban sanctuary and marveled at the colors.

Bowie stood off to the side with an electric guitar slung over his shoulder. He began to hit the first cords to one of his more obscure songs from the 1970s. As the first drumbeat hit, a drummer complete with his kit, along with another guitarist and bass player appeared behind the legend to back him up.

"Pack a pack horse and rest up here on
Black country rock
You never know you might find it here on
Black country rock
Some say the view is crazy
But you may adapt another point of view
So if it's much too hazy…"

A contented Franklin swayed to the music as he continued to watch the show. "Let's see how Durius deals with this."

Then in this reality, where everything was subject to question, both Franklin and Bowie began to change shape radically, as a rainbow of colors began to cover their bodies while their hair disappeared. As Bowie continued to sing, their skin began to develop scales from the top of their heads and on down to their feet, which mutated into 3-toed claws. When the transformation finished the entire collective identity of the Age of the Dinosaurs stood right there on the porch.

The supernatural entity previously appearing as David Bowie, now fully reptilian, slipped out his forked tongue. "Extinct my ass."

"Perish the thought," the supernatural entity previously appearing as Franklin acknowledged, as his reptilian version continued to sip from his wine glass precariously balanced on his claw like hands.

Moments after leaving Cuba in the green mist, Sean, Alicia, and Tony found themselves once again in the Admirals Ready Room on the Enterprise with klaxons ringing General Quarters. When Tony noticed Renée was not with them, he threw the half-filled glass that was still in his hand against the bulkhead.

Risking both life and limb, Alicia put her hand on his shoulder. "Easy there tiger. Why don't you take a step back until we figure out what's going on?"

Fortunately, this was enough to redirect his rage. "Fine! Let's go figure it out." Tony didn't wait for a reply as he stormed out of the room, with Sean following right behind.

"I'll stay here to see if anyone is at their post." Alicia picked up the phone to call the CIC; however, since it had not been operational for decades, decided instead to call the bridge. To her surprise, Captain Osaka's voice answered.

"You better get topside." From the tone of his voice, something had seriously freaked him out. "You are not going to believe the chaos we are in the middle of."

First Tony, now the usually unflappable Osaka sounded like he was losing it. "Captain could you calm down and tell me exactly why we are at General Quarters on a ship that hasn't been crewed for the last fifty years?"

"We're at General Quarters because there is absolutely nothing outside to give us a single reference point to determine if this ship is sitting in a body of water, or on a completely different planet."

Though Alicia could tell he was attempting to sound calm, none of what he was saying made any sense. "I'll be right there." Once she entered the corridor, she realized there wasn't anyone else around, and decided to head to the flight deck instead. "If something weird is going on, no better place to take a look," she said to herself.

When Alicia stepped through the hatch that led to the flight deck, she could see Sean and Tony standing near the starboard edge. As she walked toward them, she understood why Osaka sounded so stressed out. Instead of the ocean, the ship floated amid multi-colored waves that moved in erratic patterns. "Where in the hell did they send us this time?"

Sean turned around at the sound of her voice. "I think the more important concern at the moment than what happened to Renée is, where are we now?"

Alicia grabbed Sean's hand, and with the other pointed toward the bow of the ship. "There appears to be a rise in elevation over there about half a mile out."

Sean looked where Alicia directed and began to make out other features that seemed to rise above the swirling chaos. "That's Norfolk, I think. At least what used to be Norfolk."

Tony looked at his friend as if he had lost his mind. "Did I miss something and we traveled to another planet where we named chaos Norfolk? What in the world are you talking about?"

They remained silent for a moment, mesmerized by the craziness of their new environment, until Alicia broke the spell. "Wherever Renée is, it can't be as weird as this."

Sean was about to respond, when to his surprise, Alicia

disappeared. Before either man could react, Tony went next, followed by the disintegration of the flight deck Sean now stood alone on. As the ship faded from beneath his feet, Sean suddenly found himself floating above it.

Unlike his previous experiences shifting through time and space, this felt like diving a mile deep into an ocean of memories and emotions, each one more intense than the time he had shared memories with Alicia, no thanks to Aaron.

Then as if coming out of a tunnel, Sean found his consciousness separated from his body. He looked down upon the bridge of the Enterprise at himself, Osaka, and Tony among the rest of the bridge crew, only they were speaking German, not English. Based on the intense exchanges, and the sound of distant explosions, Sean could tell they were under attack. Then the entire ship violently shook as a series of explosions tore through her hull. Before he could comprehend the devastating consequences of what he bore witness to, the explosions reached the bridge, blowing everything and everybody to pieces.

Suddenly finding himself alone on the flight deck, Tony was about to scream out every profanity known to the sailor's dictionary when he too began to disappear. In disgust, he threw his hands up in the air, the middle finger extended on both.

Excerpt • Book V

From the Judgment In Time Series
Beyond Extinction

With a start, Alicia realized their naked state and jumped out of bed to quickly dress. "You do realize if they can pop in whenever they please, it only stands to reason our private moments are not our own."

"Well, that sure puts a damper on any future intimacy."

The disappointed little boy-look on Sean's face at the thought of a life without sex amused Alicia. "Reality is a joke. Tony and Renée are god knows where, over ten thousand members of your command unaccounted for, and you have the time to worry about sex?"

She then remembered some of the deeper corners of his mind from when they had shared minds earlier, and the lightbulb switched on. "It's a miracle men get anything done."

www.ingramcontent.com/pod-product-compliance
Lightning Source LLC
Chambersburg PA
CBHW031247120726
47905CB00002B/746